WOMEN *WHO* SLEEP
WITH ANIMALS

ALSO BY LISA NORRIS
Toy Guns

WOMEN *WHO* SLEEP WITH ANIMALS

stories

LISA NORRIS

STEPHEN F. AUSTIN STATE UNIVERSITY PRESS
2011

For information, address Stephen F. Austin State University Press, 1936 North Street, LAN 203, Nacogdoches, Texas, 75962.

sfapress.sfasu.edu

These stories have appeared in slightly altered forms in the following publications: "Dark Matter" in the *Notre Dame Review*, "Please Use the Password" in *Ascent*, "The Opening" and "Swimmers" in *South Dakota Review*, "The Lookout" in *Terrain.org*, "Scrappy" (then called "Labor Day") in *Rambler*, "Sex Toys" in *Toad* (toadthejournal.com), and "Women Who Sleep with Animals" in *Blueline*.

Cover art: Will Stauffer-Norris
Author photo: Pat Stotler

LIBRARY OF CONGRESS CATALOGING-IN-PUBLICATION DATA

Norris, Lisa,
Women who Sleep with Animals : stories / Lisa Norris.—1st ed.
p. cm.
ISBN-13: 978-1-936205-18-9

I. Title

First Edition: September 2011

For my parents Carrie and Wayne Norris
And in memory of my grandmother Margie Lee Laquatra

CONTENTS

ACKNOWLEDGMENTS

First, I would like to thank the judges who selected my manuscript and those from Stephen F. Austin State University Press who worked to edit and publish the book. In particular, I'd like to thank the press director, Kimberly Verhines, as well as her assistant, Laura McKinney.

I also appreciate the support of literary magazines that published earlier versions of the stories: "Dark Matter" in the *Notre Dame Review*, "Please Use the Password" in *Ascent*, "The Opening" and "Swimmers" in *South Dakota Review*, "The Lookout" in *Terrain. org*, "Scrappy" (then called "Labor Day") in *Rambler*, "Sex Toys" in *Toad* (toadthejournal.com), and "Women Who Sleep with Animals" in *Blueline*.

The Virginia Commission for the Arts, Virginia Tech, and Central Washington University provided financial support.

Thanks also to Tiffany and Andrew Trent who made it possible for me to watch Virginia Tech bear biologists at work. That experience inspired "Bear B45." Bill Riley provided help with facts about US Marines in Vietnam for "Please Use the Password."

The FreeRange Writers group, including Kim Barnes, Collin Hughes, Buddy Levy and Jane Varley, commented on drafts of these stories, as did Steve Abhaya Brooks, Audrey Colombe, Ed Falco, Judy Kleck Powell, Simone Poirier-Bures, Joe Powell, and Gyorgyi Voros. Particular thanks to Audrey for her tireless line edits, and to Steve for his writerly example and inspiring vision. The encouragement of these fellow writers, the care with which they read, and their persistent willingness to take time away from their own writing to look at mine is greatly appreciated.

ACKNOWLEDGMENTS

All of the characters in these stories are fictional. Probably they are projections of the author's personality. However, there are particular people and animals I found inspiring as I was writing. A group of which I am a member, called The Five Winds—including LuAnn Keener-Mikenas, Katherine Soniat, and again Gyorgyi Voros and Simone Poirier-Bures—are among these. Another dear friend, Carol Bailey, at one time cared for as many as fourteen cats and one dog. Her cat Mr. Baggins was as human an animal as I've ever met. My dog Roxy, like those who came before her (Meka, Snoopy, Sasha, Nikki, Dakota, Sage and Sterling) is a keeper of my secrets, comforter, giver and teacher.

My parents and my grandmother, Margie Lee Laquatra, taught me to love animals, both human and non-human. My English teacher mother also took me to the library and put many books into my hands featuring women (or girls) and nonhuman animals. Larry Stauffer, who was inadvertently left out of the acknowledgements of my earlier book *Toy Guns*, provided support for a horse and dogs and my writing early on. I also greatly appreciate the ongoing support of my siblings Kiel and Jody, the extended Norris family, my stepdaughter Susan and particularly my son Will who also provided the cover art.

All those animals, human and non-human, with whom I have slept provided comfort and support. I am grateful.

WOMEN *WHO* SLEEP WITH ANIMALS

DARK MATTER

So we're making love, you know, and Al is having a good time. I can tell by the way his upper lip curls and he squinches his eyes shut and gets going a little fast. He's on top, one hand between my legs, the other holding himself up. He's strong this time of year. All summer he's been doing his push-ups so he'll look okay on the beach. And I'm fine except whenever he thrusts deep, I feel this pain—not bad, but a definite pain, so I say, "You go ahead," and Al knows that's the signal I'm not going to be able to have an orgasm for one reason or another, and I'm not a faker, you know. I never fake it. That's been my rule since Day One. Some days guys can't come either. It doesn't always reflect on the other person. Could be I'm just anxious from the kid yelling or my father called or what-have-you. Whatever. You know.

Al says, "You sure, Grace?"

And I say sure.

So anyhow Al comes. And it's just light enough in the bedroom, the way the streetlight shines in, that I can see him pull out, and there on his penis—I swear we both see it at the same time—is this little blue cap, perched there on the tip, at an angle. Like it's been to town and had a few and barely managed to remember its hat before it staggered out the door.

"What the hell is that?" Al says.

And I say, "Oh my God."

We look at each other like we're looking at some kind of deformed person. My first thought is something like *Al's dick has grown a hat*. And Al's—he tells me later—is *What the hell is inside her?*

He leaps, I mean leaps, like Tarzan, up from the bed and into the bathroom, where he switches on the light to look at himself. By now the cap has fallen off, and that's what it is—a little blue cap. Like something from a tube of toothpaste.

He says, "I knew something was hurting."

I say, "You were hurting?" Because, to be honest, he didn't look like he was in pain to me.

"Just a little bit, yeah."

"Any damage?" I ask since he's examining himself, pulling his penis this way and that, up and down and sideways.

"It's a little red . . ."

And then, you know, it just kind of dawns on me that that thing was inside me. It didn't grow on Al at all. Al picked it up, like a vacuum cleaner, inside my person. Somewhere around my cervix, I guess.

I go to the gynecologist the next morning, of course, to see what else they might find inside me. I get the nurse practitioner, this woman whose son is in the same third grade class as my son. A woman who powerwalks every day on our local bike path. So healthy her skin glows. Plus she's at every PTA meeting. And here she has this good steady job and goes to all the conferences on women's health and can tell you whether you should take estrogen or not when you hit menopause and reminds you to take your calcium if you're over 35, and gives you a little mini-lecture if you gain too much weight from year to year, and her tone is always what I call the *Christian* tone, because I used to hear it all the time as a kid in Sunday school. . . this soft sweet matronizing voice that tries to hypnotize you into thinking it's not trying to tell you what to do just because it's telling you what to do nicely. You have to hate a woman like that.

But despite all this, I can't help myself. I tell her the story of how we discovered the cap. I mean I tell her the *whole* story, spare no details, including me being unable to come and feeling this little pain, like a pinch almost, and Al having no problem until he sees the little drunk with its cocked cap and gets hysterical about whether it's hurt him, and him looking at me like I've practically castrated him, and to her credit, she laughs. I imagine later Al and I become the butt of every nurse's joke. But what the hell. Among the cancer victims and the miscarriages and the herpes sufferers, I figure they could use a good laugh down at the OB-GYN's. It's all right with me if everyone knows that after twenty-one years of marriage, Al and I are still having sex.

Well, she checks me out and declares me otherwise clear of trash. No nuclear waste site, no landfill, not even a lost coin. And I have to admit, I'm a little disappointed. Who knows? There could have been a little sapling in there with magic fruit; loaves and fishes; watermelon vines from all those seeds I swallowed when I was a kid—okay, I know, your stomach doesn't connect to your uterus, but what the hell, you don't find a little blue cap on a penis everyday either.

But it turns out all I have is this ordinary muscular space inside me where I just so happened to carry a little blue cap that came from one of those deals you inject into yourself when you have a yeast infection.

"The directions tell you to remove the cap before inserting," the nurse practitioner tells me.

Whoops.

When I get home Al's already changed out of his suit and tie, and he's sitting tragically on the lawn under the maple tree, looking at the wreckage of a garden box. He's wearing his bright orange Beachmasters 5K T-shirt, his khaki shorts, his white crew socks and holey sneakers. He's a big man, all hairy arms and legs, and he's sitting with his elbows resting on his knees, head bowed, so the dome of his head reflects the evening sun. He's laid the first couple of logs, hammered them together, no problem, but the third log is a good foot shorter than the rest: it doesn't fit.

"Trouble?" I ask.

"I measured it and measured it," he says.

I put a hand on his shoulder. "I believe you."

"It kept coming out different. Every time."

I pick up the measuring tape, note that one side's calibrated in centimeters, the other in inches. "I can understand that."

"So finally I got tired of it, and I just cut."

I kiss the top of his head. "It's just a little setback."

But Al tightens his jaw, and I know he's going to be no kind of company until the box is built and built right. Then there will be the dog door and the skyfort roof. It could be a long summer.

"Well I found out what the blue cap was," I tell him. "And you were right, it's nothing to do with you."

"Sure," he says, without conviction.

The next morning, I reach over him to the magazine on his nightstand. He likes to read science. I point to the picture of a spaceship, then reach into his pajama pants. "We could pretend he's an astronaut." I pull a condom out of the drawer. "We could even dress him in his spacesuit."

We both look at the little peanut in my hand.

"You're not still stressing over the cap," I say.

Al ducks his head. "It's like the thing at the back of the closet that you knew was going to get you, and then it does. Just give me a little time."

"It's been a week."

"After Shawn was born, you wanted a month or so."

"I had stitches."

Al clears his throat, then pulls the covers up over his chest. He raises his knees to make a place for his magazine to rest.

"Don't ignore me."

Al points to a page in the magazine. "Look at this, hon. Dark matter."

"Dark matter."

"Right," Al says. "They think black holes are made of this stuff. They think maybe it holds together the universe."

"And they don't know what it is?"

"Nope."

"So what's new?" I ask Al. "They didn't know what it was before. They don't know now. They could just as well call it Elmer's glue."

"You're missing the point."

I get up and go to the bathroom. When I come back, I pull on my jeans. In the mirror, though, I catch Al looking up from his magazine at my tits, which are—if I say so myself—two of my best features. I walk over to the bed and pull his face right into them. "Dark matter," I say. He closes his eyes and burrows into me like a gigantic child.

At the elementary school, our son Shawn runs onto the field to join his soccer team, and who do I see but the nurse practitioner in her tidy pink shorts and bright white walking shoes, her blonde bob curling under at her chin. "Grace." She grins, revealing a black speck caught between her two front teeth. "No more surprises, I hope?"

I focus on the speck—a sesame seed, I think—glad (who can help it?) to see this public display of a foreign body lodged in someone else's anatomy.

"As a matter of fact, yes."

It's one of those humid Virginia afternoons when I can hardly breathe, but the nurse—Ruth is her name—looks as cool as if she's still in her air-conditioned office. I touch her elbow. "I hate to bother you with it when you're not on duty."

She waves a hand between us.

"It's not like I'm going to have you examine me or anything."

She laughs, the seed dark with spittle and lodged firmly.

I lower my voice. "It's my husband. Ever since the, you know, cap thing, he won't—" I spread my hands.

"He doesn't want to or he can't?"

"Well, one kind of leads to the other."

She fingers the curl at her chin.

"So what do you do with a guy like that?" I ask her.

She turns toward the field where our sons are running up and down in a senseless way between the goals after a small round object. "He probably needs to feel like he's in control. You're going to have to wait until he takes the initiative. Why not romance him a little? But don't be too obvious." She waggles a finger like a teacher saying *Naughty, naughty*, and grins.

"By the way, you've got a little something right here," I tell her, indicating my front teeth. "A sesame seed, maybe."

I leave her red in the face, her thumbnail in her mouth, working to remove the offending body.

I buy a bottle of Jack Daniels and a couple of candles. I study the selection at the video stores and come home with Jessica Lange. That's the way I think of it, I've got Jessica Lange on the seat next to me in the car on the way home. I'm say-ing Jessica, sweetheart, my husband's crazy about you, and tonight, I need you to do me a favor. If Al wants to kiss my mouth and imagine Jessica's, at this point it's all the same to me. When I get home, I find Al in the middle of what used to be the lawn, turning up shovels of dirt.

"What the hell are you doing?"

"I want to put another garden in here."

"What about the other one? the raised beds and the box and all that?"

"Well, sure."

"Sure what?"

"Sure I'll finish that up."

"When?"

Al puts a foot on the shovel and pushes it into the dirt, then wipes his hands on his shorts and glares at me. "Look, I'm tired of mowing this lawn week after week. I just want to get rid of it."

"We could have the whole thing paved."

"Very funny."

"Hon." I sidle up to him, kiss his grimy cheek. "Look who I got for you to watch tonight." I hold up the video in a teasing way.

Al looks off toward the neighbor's yard, then shakes his head. "Look at that grass. Always immaculate."

I pick up a dandelion, blow the white fluff in his face.

Later Al kicks back in the recliner, leaving me alone on the couch. He makes himself comfortable, afghan over his lap, sipping on his drink. "This is really nice, hon. Just you and me. No shovels or lawnmowers or circular saws or anything." The candles flicker on the coffee table between us. Al blows me a kiss. We get to watching the movie—I'm thinking I'll be pa-tient, let Al make the first move. Then, just as Jessica's thrown onto the bed and Dennis Quaid, playing the all-American football hero, is finding his way under her dress, I hear a rasping sound coming from the direction of my husband. I notice under the afghan, his hand is cupped over his crotch, as if, even in his sleep, to ward off invasion.

Al replaces the short log on the garden box and makes another log's worth of progress. Weeds have begun to take hold in the patch of lawn he dug up, and there's a gaping hole in the basement door, waiting for the dog flap to be installed. There's still no roof on the sky fort. Shawn took some paperback books out there to read and came in complaining a few days later they were all ruined in the rain.

"I should stay home and work on my projects," Al protests when I ask him to spend the day at the beach.

"Take a break," I say. "Shawn's spending the day over at Ronnie's."

"So it's just you and me?"

"Right."

He runs a hand over the naked top of his head, as if he's searching for the lost hair, which used to be one of his best features. He looks out the window across the ploughed-up yard, checking out our white-haired neighbor, Sam McAllister, out on his riding mower, wearing shin-length trouser socks, penny loafers, shorts and a golf shirt. His wife, dressed in a flowered moo-moo, her hair sprayed in place, is out with the edger, the skin flapping under her bare arms.

Al gestures helplessly. "What can it be like to live like that?"

"Like what?"

"Everything in order."

"Come on. They're retired. What else do they have to do?"

"What about the Pinellis? They both work full-time. And look at their place."

"They have a gardener."

"I'm bringing down the neighborhood."

"Like hell."

"Look around you." Al gestures out the window at the half-dug lawn, the unroofed sky fort, etc. "I can't do anything right."

"Think about Tate's yard, that disaster area over there on the corner."

"Tate's a drunk."

"And you're not."

"That's true." He strokes his chin. "So now instead of saying *There but for the grace of God go I*, I'm saying, *thank God I'm better than that sot?*"

"Whatever works."

Salt air, heat on the skin, rhythm of the waves, near-naked bodies. I'm hoping the beach'll work some magic on Al, at least get him out of his lawn snit. I hold my straw hat with one hand and carry the picnic basket with the other. We've parked at 61st Street, a neighborhood far from the boardwalk and the tourists. It's a clear day, breezy, perfect. There's a red-suited blonde guy in the lifeguard stand, a few scattered towels with sleeping bodies. One umbrella. A radio playing country-western. Plenty of room.

I put down the picnic basket to help Al stretch the bed-sheet, a faded pink floral. "We made Shawn on this sheet."

"You're telling me you remember the particular sheet?" He pulls out a paperback, some book by Stephen Hawking. *A Brief History of Time*.

"Yeah well." I pop my fingers against the cover of his book "Some of us live a little closer to earth than others." I unwrap a chocolate and slide it between my lips. "Want one?"

I lie back on the sheet and close my eyes. The sun warms my skin. I can still taste the chocolate left on my tongue. A breeze from the water keeps me from broiling, bringing the smells of salt and suntan lotion. Waves thrum against the shore. Little kids scream their screams of thrill and delight as they play in the surf. "Remember when Shawn used to scream like that?"

"Um-hm."

"I wouldn't trade that."

"No. But sometimes I wonder if I'd trade the job. The house. The yard. Every week taking out the garbage. Then I die."

I open the picnic basket, chock full of food I read in the newspaper's *Extra* section would stimulate the libido. "Have an oyster."

"What's it all add up to? Don't you think about that?"

"Not much."

"Don't you want to understand it?"

Though my eyes are closed, I can feel Al leaning on one elbow, wanting something from me. I roll onto my side so my suit slides off just enough to reveal some flesh in Al's direction.

"I'm sorry, hon," he says. "Here you've brought me this nice picnic and we're alone on the beach, and all I can think about is how come if the universe is expanding, I feel so closed in?"

Alone in front of the mirror, I check out my suntan. The skin puckers and folds where it used to be nice and tight around my waist. I remember the green-eyed girl with the smooth complexion, but now I see a blotchy-skinned woman with pouches under her eyes. Al says according to the Second Law of Thermodynamics, all things tend to disorder. No shit. I imagine my body as if it's in one of those time-lapse videos they do of flowers on nature shows. The flowers blossom and get beautiful. But I'm past that prime. In my video, my body shrinks.

My scalp shows through my thinning hair. My tits sag to my waist. Finally I'm pissing into a bedpan and breathing through a tank. Then I get cremated and scattered back into the earth, and I have to wonder, of course, what it all means. If there's something, dark matter or what-have-you, that holds things together, don't I want it to hold me together? And what about me and Al?

Monday afternoon, I run the vacuum, like I do week after week. That's after I clean the toilet bowls and sink basins, do the floors and bed linens; clean the oven, the refrigerator, and the dishes. I think about black holes, the way they're supposed to suck things up or pull things down, like a drain. I run over a bobby pin and it makes an awful sound, rattling around inside the machine. The words *dark matter* feel like they're doing the same thing in my head, jiggling around like a line from a song. *Dark matter, dark matter. Hey Jude, don't let it down. Ridin' through the desert on a horse with no name . . .*

The bobby pin catches inside the machine, making it buzz. I switch it off, turn it, and with the flat of my palm, I roll the rollers that pick up lint from the carpet, hoping the bobby pin will fall out. I try to imagine what it would be like if the rollers were removed and an opening appeared just the size of the most sensitive part of my anatomy. What if I had the option of plunging that part into the opening, not knowing what was beyond? *We have an alien in the engine room, Scotty.*

Vera McAllister, borrowing a cup of sugar. She's got a painted scarf tied over her curlers, and she's dressed in knee-length shorts and a sleeveless blouse with a collar. Her face is dry as paper from cooking herself at the beach. She talks like a chipping bird.

"Poor-Sam-can't-do-anything-anymore. But-sit-on-that-ridin'-mower. It's-up-to-me-to-weed-and-edge-and-all-the-rest. And-it's-just-too-much. So-we've-about-decided-to-sell-out. Move-to-a-retirement-home."

Al drives in just as Vera's leaving, giving her a wave and a toot from the red Taurus with the spoiler he wanted to make him feel like all hope for the TransAm he really wanted was not yet lost. Shawn, playing in the sky fort, sends a spray of water from his XP 110 plastic gun to greet his father. Al acts like he's shot and staggers across the lawn. Or should I say, dirt.

"You're home early," I observe when he comes in the door.

He gives me the usual cheek peck, slides off his suit jacket, loosens his tie, gets a beer out of the refrigerator. "I took a few days off."

"By choice?"

"I'm going to stay home and get some things finished."

"Really." I imagine the cursing, the dirt tracked across my clean floor. "Well good." I take out a beer for myself as I digest the news of this week's interruption. When I go to bed that night, as usual these days, Al makes an excuse to watch TV until after I'm asleep.

Next day he's out there first thing in the morning wrestling big sheets of roofing out to the sky fort. It's my day to wash sheets. There's a nice breeze from the bay that would dry them fast on the line. But the plastic roofing looks like some live thing trying to consume my husband. It bends around him as he stands on the ladder, trying to tack it to the rafters he's nailed in place. I think about the way he staggered across the lawn when Shawn pretended to squirt him from the sky fort. I think about how his big hands on my skin make me feel like a girl, no matter how fat I get. Though he's not a man for odd jobs, my Al—that sweetheart—has taken vacation days to putter around the house. So I go out to help. I'm standing in the sky fort holding onto the roofing, Al on staple gun duty, when we hear the sirens wailing right down our street and see the ambulance pull into the McAllisters' driveway.

We stop what we're doing to watch. The white-coated crew wheels Sam into the ambulance while Vera, still in her scarf and curlers, follows quickly behind.

We don't have to ask what happened when we see the traffic in and out of the McAllister place the next day. People with out-of-town license plates bear cakes and casseroles across the perfect lawn. From our upstairs window I watch one woman's spiked heels sink into the sod. I want to shout at her to use the sidewalk. Instead I get on the scale in the bathroom. I'm five-foot-seven, and I weigh 148. Oh good Christ. I turn sideways and note the belly, the thighs. In the pale light, I can see the faint blue and purple veins mottling the surface of my legs. My hair, despite the sun at the beach, still needs highlighting.

When I get down the stairs, there's flesh of my flesh, blood of my blood, dressed in black soccer shorts and a dinosaur T-shirt, eating his Fruit Loops while his dad reads the paper. Shawn's skin fits tightly over his small muscles. His arms are covered in a soft blonde fuzz.

I fix a piece of toast and sit nursing my coffee, watching Shawn slurp the cereal into his freckled face. Milk dribbles out the sides of his mouth, but if, this morning, we were in a movie, he'd be the one bathed in a yellow light, shot through a soft filter. I want to crumple Al's newspaper and say to him, yeah, a little blue cap came out of me, but look what else. I get up and brush crumbs from my lap and start banging around in the kitchen cabinets.

"Grace?" Al says. "What's up?"

"I'm going to bake today. That's what."

"More chocolate chip cookies?" Shawn asks.

"You still have some left. Today it's going to be something for Vera. Banana bread maybe." As if food will help.

Al folds up the paper. "That's nice of you."

We hear the toot of a car horn out the door, Shawn's signal

that his ride to soccer practice has arrived and, because of the traffic at the McAllisters', can't get into the driveway. He shouts his goodbyes as he slams the front door.

Al comes up behind me, kisses my shoulder.

I break his hold, sponging the counters. "Have you noticed what a wreck everything is? The grime on the windows, the food in the drain, the handprints on the walls . . . The other day, the thing you said about taking out the garbage, you were right."

"What'd I say?"

"We take out the garbage, then we die."

"You didn't have enough breakfast, hon. All you had was a piece of toast."

"What do you think was the last thing they talked about?"

"Who?"

I nod toward the McAllisters. "Do you think it was that the grass was too long? Or there were dirty streaks on the windows?" I feel the knot in my belly gushing up to my throat.

Al picks at the grime on the handle of the refrigerator.

"He was more bonded to the goddamn lawn than he was to Vera," I say.

"Hon—"

"If he wasn't dead before, he is now."

Al opens the refrigerator door, peers in, then slams it closed. He rubs the top of his head. "I don't want us winding up like Al and Vera anymore than you do."

I look out the window toward the half-roofed sky fort, then lean into him for a hug. "So what do we do?"

I feel his breath on my neck, his lips on my earlobe. His fingers push under my robe, warming my breasts. "Maybe think about what's underneath."

Then lo and behold, I feel his little captain coming to attention. When I turn around, we kiss each other's mouths like kids in the backseat of a Chevy. Al fumbles with his belt, and

I throw off my robe. Next thing you know, I'm on the cold tile floor. I look toward the sliding glass door, where there's grime caught in the runner. I can feel Al then, quivering inside me like he halfway wants to back out. I say, "You go ahead," but he says, "Not without you." I tighten my grip, my fingers sliding on his back, over moles and muscles as familiar to me as my own. "Al," I say. This time there's no pinch, so I know there will be no little blue cap riding the top of his penis like a cowboy halfway off a bronc. Only my husband pushing himself into whatever's inside me, my arms and legs wrapping around him, each of lost in the other one's offering, both of us holding on.

BEAR B-45

In the truck, Eva pushes the driver's seat all the way back to accommodate her long legs but still feels cramped, and her stomach churns, acidic with bad coffee. Her father has called, just an hour ago, to say her mother is in the hospital again. He hasn't said *this could be it*. She tries not to think about *it*, but she's still debating whether she should turn the truck around, drop off the other women, and head for DC, five hours northeast, or keep driving toward the bear. Pastures on either side of the road are still white and frozen. The two other women on the bench seat of the truck aren't speaking right now. Eva's clothing—long johns, jeans, shirt, sweater—makes her feel mummified, and her back hurts. Maybe a hike in the frosty woods will loosen her up. Collecting her data will focus her attention on something besides the pain, though if her mother is in pain, why shouldn't Eva be, too?

Beyond the stream-cut valley, she plans to turn onto a Forest Service road and take a trail up the mountain to the den of bear B45. The white truck with its maroon university logo is hers for the day. For now, she's holding it steady between Appalachian ridges on the plowed road. It's the usual road—one she frequently travels to her study area. The other two women met her where it intersects the main highway, leaving their cars parked at the trailer that doubles as a post office. Now, a mile further into the valley, smoke curls from the chimneys of farmhouses, trailers, brick ranchers. Snow brightens the open spaces between an occasional church or country store. Eva's technician, Dawna, holds her childlike body on a small island of vinyl between her boss and Ronelle, who is built like a Sumo wrestler. The cab smells of coffee—Ronelle brought a thermos and three Styrofoam cups, as well as a bag of powdered donuts.

"Did you remember the jab stick?" Eva asks Ronelle.

"Did I remember the jab stick?" Ronelle's many braids rustle over the fabric of her green parka as she shifts her weight off the passenger door, puts her hand on the heater vent, and adjusts the air. She spreads her legs to accommodate her belly, pushes her granny glasses up to the bridge of her nose. "You question my competence?"

Dawna says, "I got the dart gun." She looks lost inside her maroon jacket, like a little girl dressed up in her father's clothing. Her front teeth jut in a face unremarkable except for eyebrows and eyelashes so blonde they can barely be seen. Her round blue eyes are naked. Her expression's sour, as it has been ever since she lost her baby.

"Good," Eva says. We can put her out." She pictures bear B45 harmless in a tranquilized torpor. The bear is now six years old. When they measured her two winters earlier, she was five feet five inches from nose to tail, weighed 160 lbs., and had three cubs. Two survived and were granted independence, so likely she'll have newborns in the den with her now. So Eva and Ronelle hope, though Eva suspects that Dawna hasn't held a baby *anything* since she found her daughter dead in the crib two months ago. Lately Dawna's been unusually quiet, answering *how are you*—which she used to deflect by saying, *how's your own self*—with only with a nod. The truck rounds a curve, Ronelle's leg bumps Dawna's, and Eva sees Dawna jerk herself away from the touch.

Eva leans forward in her seat, arching her back, trying to work out the ache. She holds her shoulders in a forward hunch—a tall woman who wishes to be shorter. She has a long narrow nose, thin lips, and a high forehead. She pulls her bone-straight hair back into a ponytail. Parallel lines deepen between her brows as she reminds herself to breathe, but when she breathes too deeply, the pinched nerve stabs, and whenever it does, she thinks of her mother.

The last time they talked, she wished her mother a happy birthday, to which her mother replied, "If I'm lucky, this'll be the last. Everything hurts." Eva, phone pressed to her ear as she sat looking at her computer, imagined her mother sitting on the couch in pressed slacks and a cashmere sweater, gray hair of her wig curling at her chin, blue veins standing out on her hands.

"What about Dad and me?"

She heard her mother swallow, knew she was holding a wine glass. "You'd be better off."

"You know we don't believe that."

Eva lets up on the gas as they approach a sign for *Huffman*.

In the truck, Dawna nods toward the horizon. "My daddy grew up out here."

"Did he have a nice front porch like that one?" Ronelle

points to a two-story farmhouse with an empty rocking chair by the front door.

"He lived in a," Dawna pauses, then lets out a hiss of breath, "trailer," as if she's struggling not to be ashamed. Eva imagines she's heard plenty of people talk about *rednecks* and *trailer trash*. "Bobby and me? After I got this technician job, we found us a *real* house in Giles County, you know, right on a creek. We thought it'd be a good place to raise up our—" She puts her face in her hands.

Ronelle touches Dawna's arm, "We heard what happened."

Dawna shrugs her off.

"There's Kleenex in the glove compartment," Eva says.

Ronelle flips it open with her free hand, pulls out a tissue and gives it to Dawna, who snatches it and keeps her head down.

Eva says, "My mother lost a baby, too. Before I was born. She was," her voice pauses, "they say she was never the same after, but I never knew her before. He would have been my big brother."

"At least she had another one. She had you," Ronelle says.

"She was sad anyway. Ever since I can remember. She tried to drink it away. Right now, she's in the hospital. My dad called me last night."

"Wasn't she in the hospital last month, too?" Ronelle asks.

"Cancer," Eva says. "Depression all her life. Fibromyalgia. One suicide attempt." She hears the sharp intake of Dawna's breath, as if in a sob. "Now cancer."

She lifts a hand to touch Dawna's leg but feels Dawna's refusal in the way Dawna holds her body, tight, knees drawn up almost to the dashboard, so Eva returns her hand to the steering wheel without making contact. "Of course, that doesn't have to be your story."

Dawna clenches the dashboard with both hands.

"My mother's a special case," Eva continues. "Sometimes I

think she loves her pain."

Into her hands, Dawna says, "That's just crazy."

The few houses disappear. Pastures open up to either side of the road again, rising to foothills and weathered ridges topped by skeletal hardwoods. "Leaving Huffman behind," Ronelle says, as if it's a relief.

Dawna looks behind her out the back window. "Huffmans." She blows her nose. "They *own* this valley. When I was growing up here, Billy Huffman used to call my girlfriend Twila the N word and me the N word lover." She faces the front again. "So I stopped bein' her friend."

Eva glances toward Ronelle, who looks pointedly out the window, away from the other women. "Times have changed," Eva says, quickly. "We elected Obama."

"Oh yeah. That changes *every*thing," Ronelle says.

"Well, it's a start," Eva says. "Like getting your PhD."

Ronelle rolls her eyes. "Just like the boss."

As Eva knows, Ronelle will defend her dissertation in the Spring. Her boyfriend O'Keesa, getting his doctorate in Sociology, is a year behind her. All Ronelle needs to finish her research is the data. Bear B45 and her cubs will provide the last of it. Touching bears is a thrill in itself, but Ronelle has told Eva that touching bears is also her ticket to respect and job security.

The truck plunges ahead into the bright morning, tires humming on dry asphalt. They don't speak until Ronelle points to a Forest Service road sign. "That's it, right?"

Eva nods, slows the truck, turns and engages the four-wheel-drive. "Here's the trail to pay dirt. Hold on." She guns the engine to power the truck up the unplowed grade.

At the top, where the road levels out, Eva says, "We just have to find the first flagged tree." She points to the dash in front of Ronelle who slides a folded piece of paper into her lap and smoothes it to read.

"Three point two miles from the highway, then left, then another mile, then park by the big yellow poplar," Ronelle says. "It's a ground den, right?"

"That's why we have the little squirrel along." Eva nods toward Dawna.

"Bobby? He thinks I'm crazy to go crawlin into a bear den," Dawna says.

Eva keeps her eyes fixed on the road. The back end is weighted with sand, but the truck slides toward the road's edge when she hits an icy patch. "Jesus," she says. The other women jolt toward Eva. Dawna jabs Ronelle with an elbow to get her to move away.

"Ouch. Easy, girl." Ronelle grabs the dash. "Maybe we *are* crazy. Going up this road."

"I don't think so," Eva says. "And believe me, I know." She blinks away a vision of her mother sitting on the edge of her bed in a hospital gown. "The den won't be dangerous. I'll dart the bear before anybody else goes in. I'm really the only one at risk."

Dawna makes a pistol with her forefinger and thumb, aims it out the windshield and narrows her eyes. "I feel like shootin' something. You should let me do it. Pow."

Ronelle makes her voice sound like an announcer's. "The good Dr. Eva will keep us from harm."

Dawna blows on her forefinger as if to cool her revolver, lowers it into her lap, but keeps the forefinger out, aimed at Ronelle.

"That's it." Eva slows the truck to negotiate a hairpin curve. She still feels the pain in her back with each jab, as well as a numbness and haze between herself and the material world. Is having one's parent on her deathbed like being inebriated? Should she have a designated driver? When the road straightens out, she takes another swig of coffee. "Once the mama's out, we don't have to worry."

"That's when I crawl in and get the cubs," Dawna says.

"Like Sharon showed you," Ronelle says.

"She said there wasn't nothing to it."

"What's Sharon got?" Eva asks.

"Flu," Ronelle says. "But you were available," she says to Dawna. "I sure wasn't going to fit."

"No *lie.* " Dawna's eyes narrow, her lips thin. Eva wonders if Ronelle is offended, but Ronelle ignores Dawna, unwraps a pack of Lifesavers, and pops one into her mouth. Eva can smell it—cherry.

A few more jolts, then Eva parks in front of a big oak tree belted with a pink ribbon.

Outside, they pull backpacks from the pick-up. Eva checks the supplies: Ronelle carries the radio transmitter, Eva the syringes and vials of tranquilizer and jab stick. Dawna has the dart gun, scale, and tattooing equipment. Dawna eyes their coats as if she wants one for herself. Ronelle wears a cashmere scarf around her neck, and Eva has on down mittens.

"I brought an extra down vest," Eva says, considering Dawna's thin coat. "It'll swallow you up, but it might be warmer."

Dawna clasps her hands together, hiding the holes in her gloves. "Ya'll are talking to a *mountain* woman."

Eva frowns. "Even *mountain* women get hypothermia."

Ronelle fishes in her pockets, pulls out a wrapped candy bar. "Anybody for chocolate?"

"My grandpa wouldn't let me take chocolate from no colored woman." Dawna sniffs. "He used to say, 'That might be sweet, but ya'll don't know where it's been.'" She shows her teeth, holds out a palm anyway.

Ronelle jerks the candy away from her. "Not funny."

Eva wants to redirect the conversation. "How'd you two get into bears anyway?" It's an effort to keep her tone light, but if this is the way she's going to go instead of reversing her direction to sit by her mother, she must turn her crew toward their purpose.

"Discovery channel," Ronelle says.

Dawna snarls, "TV bears." She makes a face and shakes her head. "You see a bear running from the dogs like I did when I went hunting with my daddy—now *that's* real."

"Oh yeah." Ronelle rolls her eyes. "Just like nature intended."

"Tell that to the dogs." Dawna hawks and spits. "Anyway, what do you know about it? There's people out here that don't eat unless they shoot their dinners."

"How do they afford the guns and ammo? The big trucks, the dogs, the walkie-talkies and all that other shit?" Ronelle asks.

"'Cause they *ain't* subscribing to the Discovery Channel," Dawna says.

Ronelle starts to object, but Eva presses her forearm, turning her back on Dawna. She lets her eyes plead with Ronelle for peace. "Let's get to work."

2.

They hike in single file, Eva leading. Leafless branches cast sharp shadows on the snowy floor. Once in a while, Eva lifts a sleeve to her dripping nose. Some of her claustrophobia has lifted since they got out of the truck, but her limbs still feel heavy, her back throbs, as if her body's draped with invisible weights.

Her father's call awakened her that morning. She pictured him on the other end, balding head in one palm, angular body folded, still wearing—as he told her—pajama pants and an overcoat after he returned from the hospital where he'd taken

Eva's mother in the wee hours.

"Dad." Eva held the phone to her ear, looked out the window by her bed. The air was black. "What can I do?"

Her father breathed as if the mere act of picking up the phone had been an exertion. "It's not in your hands."

"I could get there by tonight."

"No."

"But I want to—"

"You know what you can do for me?" The antique clock (she pictured it on the mantel) chimed on the hour. "Just one thing, that's all I need. Take pleasure in your own life—please."

"How am I supposed to do that?"

"You only have so much time," her father said. "I know how that is." She thought of him at his computer in the apartment late at night, reviewing columns of numbers. He was a genetics professor. As a girl, she'd sat on his lap some nights and watched him work after her mother had drunk herself into a stupor and gone to bed.

"Aren't you and Mother more important?"

Her father was quiet. Maybe he was moved. "I need someone to live a normal life," he said quietly. "I want it to be you."

In the woods, Eva hears the distant tapping of a woodpecker, the high-pitched chipping of the juncos that fly from branches ahead of her. The air smells clean. She's studied ecology and thought about interrelationships between moisture and soil, temperature and plants. Hemlocks and rhododendrons prosper by the creeks, and certain pines grow on the south slopes, where the soil is drier and there's always more sun. The trees, familiar as old friends whose names and natural histories she knows well, offer comfort, despite the cold. *Quercus alba. Pinus concolor.* She breathes deeply, sees her mother's composed face, fully made up—always with the eyeliner, lipstick, fake eyelashes—and feels her back clench. She halts, steadying herself against the trunk of a paper birch. *Betula papyrifera.*

Dawna catches up to her, leans against a tree trunk, and looks back down the trail. "Too bad we have to wait for the *help.*"

Eva hears the slur, shakes her head, decides to ignore it. "She's got more load to carry than we do." They watch Ronelle labor up the slope. Her body pitches forward as she lifts each thick leg, eyes on the ground.

Dawna shivers. She tucks her hands under her armpits, stomping her feet to stay warm. "Don't ask me to feel sorry for her. *She's* the one eating candy."

Maybe it'll be better, Eva thinks, if she keeps the two women apart. "Go on up," she says to Dawna. "You'll be warmer that way. Just follow the ribbons."

By the time Ronelle arrives, Dawna has disappeared around the next switchback.

"I'm sweating." Ronelle slips her pack off her shoulders, removes her jacket, and ties it around her waist. "What is it, another couple miles?"

Eva nods.

"If it's the same den she had last year, we have to go up over that ridge, right?" Ronelle points ahead and up the trail toward the horizon line, interrupted by what appears to be a mountaintop.

"We're not seeing the top yet," Eva says. "You know how that is."

"As we approach, the destination recedes." Ronelle gazes upslope. "You really think that girl's gonna do okay in the den?" Ronelle asked.

"She's a *mountain* woman."

"I miss the other girl. Sharon. Dawna's an asshole."

Eva lets the words hang. "Look, I don't want to make excuses for her, but I heard she's still paying for her baby's funeral."

"So give her a donation. Don't take her on a scientific expedition."

"Who else did we have?" She shifts her weight, moaning, her palm to her back.

"What's the problem?" Ronelle looks at her.

Eva lowers her torso from the waist, feels the pull in her hamstrings. "Pinched nerve."

Ronelle rolls her eyes. "The crippled and the racist."

They round a switchback where a game trail leaves the path to cut through the trees toward a cliff. Dawna stands at the cliff's edge, maroon jacket flapping from her thin frame, arms outstretched. She teeters, appears to lose her balance, then pitches forward. Eva's heart skids, but Dawna doesn't disappear over the edge. Instead, her head drops a foot, but her body remains upright, and she turns toward them, her laughter sounding like something between a cackle and a sob. Now Eva understands there's a ledge beneath Dawna that Eva and Ronelle are unable to see.

"You little shit!" Ronelle says. "You scared the crap out of me."

Dawna says, "Ya'll got no sense of humor. What do you take me for—crazy?" She looks at Ronelle's beefy face, her expensive boots. "I ain't no crazier than a coon." Ronelle's face collapses into hurt.

Eva holds up a hand as if to stop Dawna and opens her mouth to speak as Ronelle advances, but Dawna picks up her pack and skitters onto the trail, taking a big detour through the brush to avoid Eva and Ronelle. She doesn't speak or look back, and soon she's out of sight.

"Jesus," Eva says. "I'm really sorry."

"You know, I could walk off this mountain right now and leave you alone with her."

"I wouldn't blame you." Eva makes her voice sound even,

though Ronelle's departure would mean the end of the expedition.

"You need me worse than you need her."

Eva imagines her own half-written paper on her desk at home. The sample size is still too small. Bear B45 and her cubs are significant to *her* study as well as Ronelle's. Ronelle is a co-author. She and Ronelle have already published some of the preliminary data, and Ronelle has the numbers on her computer—a computer to which Eva doesn't have access. What if she were alone with Dawna when the bear came out of her stupor? Any number of things could go wrong. "If there are problems, she won't know how to—"

"Right."

Eva steps forward, slides on a patch of ice, and barely recovers. Pain stabs in her back. "Shit." She rests her weight against a tree, letting the spasm subside.

Ronelle turns her face to the sky. "Sweet fucken Jesus. Why me?"

3.

They hike another mile through the leafless hardwoods, losing their view of the valley floor as the trail meanders over the ridge and down into a hollow. Rhododendrons grow along the banks of a trickling creek, their leaves wilting among pointed icicles.

"There she is," Eva says.

Dawna's maroon jacket moves through the trees. She walks in circles, hands in her pockets to keep warm. "What took ya'll so long?" she asks. "I ran out a ribbons here." She jerks her chin toward a tree tied with a pink ribbon. Her baseball cap swivels as she looks around the clearing. "Where's the den?"

Eva points to a fallen log against which brush piles in a

tangle of limbs and leaves. "Under there."

They unpack the gear, organizing it so when they bring the cubs out of the den, their measurements will be efficient. Ronelle and Dawna avoid eye contact, making wide arcs around each other, stiff-legged, like dogs circling with raised hackles before they leap snarling into a fight.

After they clear brush away from the den's entrance, Eva, on her knees, shines the flashlight into the tunnel. "I don't know if I'll be able to make that first jab."

Ronelle hands her a spade and headlamp. "Sure your back can take this?"

"We'll see."

Dawna says, "You want me to crawl in there first, I'll do it. It's got to be warmer than it is out here." She stamps her feet and blows on her fingertips.

"You should've taken that extra vest," Ronelle says.

Dawna sneers. "You people know all about handouts."

Ronelle sets her jaw, reaches into a pocket, and takes out a caramel. She unwraps it slowly, sliding it into her mouth as if to taunt Dawna.

Eva just wants to get the job done. "Hand me the jab stick."

"It's in the blue pack," Ronelle nods toward Dawna. The pack is at Dawna's feet, but Dawna lifts her chin and kicks the pack toward Ronelle.

Eva lurches for the pack before Ronelle can react—though it costs her a sickening flash of pain, and then, all business, she says, "Ronelle, you spot me here." She indicates the ground in front of the den.

Ronelle glares at nothing, her jaw set.

"Dawna, take inventory of the vegetation."

Dawna swivels her head. "Where at?"

"Just right here." Eva waves her arms. "A quarter-acre plot with the den at the center."

Dawna looks at her hands.

"The faster we work, the sooner we get back to the warm truck," Eva says.

Scowling, Dawna kneels to dig through her pack for the clipboard and measuring equipment.

Eva pushes into the tunnel, arms in front of her like a diver's. It's a relief to get the project moving, immersing herself in the quiet earth. She smells the musk of bear, feels her heartbeat quicken.

Propelling herself with the toes of her feet, she inches along on her belly. The tunnel narrows soon enough, jamming against her shoulders. Its angle downward, she estimates, is about 30 degrees, so blood rushes to her head, her pulse sounds in her ears. She's really too big for the space. If Sharon had been with them, Eva would have given her the job. She has to push herself forward with her toes, press against the earth with her shoulders, sometimes dig into the dirt with her fingernails to pull herself along. Maybe she should've called this expedition off. It's so close inside the tunnel, she can barely breathe, and her back feels weak, like it could go any minute. But after a few minutes of crawling, she sees, in the light from her headlamp, the mother bear's open eyes, and that's her reward.

Eva works the jab stick down toward the den, a cavern big enough for her to turn around in, lined with grass and pine needles. She can make out three cubs. Bear B45 blinks in the beam of the flashlight. She's lethargic. She's given birth here and eaten the afterbirth. If there were stillbirths, she's ingested those, too. She's survived through several months of winter, not once going out for food or water. It's a miracle of biology, the way her metabolism slows almost to nothing as new life emerges from her, beneath the earth. Eva takes only a moment, though, to marvel, aware that she must tranquilize the sow before the bear's heartbeat increases. She pushes the jab stick through the narrow part of the tunnel, but it's so tight that she can't see beyond it to aim. She bends her elbow to pull it back toward her, looks again with her light through the opening. Now the sow's moving, gathering herself.

She can almost see the words emblazoned in her mind, *Stay calm*. Fear in any form, she knows, can set a predator off.

Bear B45 clicks her teeth at Eva. She huffs.

Eva inches backward, jab stick still before her like the spear of an underwater diver, but unlike a diver, she's not weightless inside the tunnel: neurons fire along her spinal cord like small nuclear bombs, exploding invisibly, searing. She pushes through the pain, squirming backward, uphill, in reverse, toward the tunnel's opening. Though she can't see into the den anymore, she knows the bear's metabolism is speeding up. She once read about a bear whose heartbeat went from 8 beats a minute to 180 in the space of just a few minutes.

Is she making progress in the dark? Eva can't tell. When she bends her knees, her feet press against the roof of the tunnel. Not yet. She lowers them and inches backward some more. The tunnel lightens. Almost there. Are Ronelle and Dawna watching? Is Ronelle spotting Eva as Eva'd asked? Hopeful, she pushes herself backward, but her shoulders catch, too big for the narrow opening.

She struggles on her belly, kicking her feet like a kid having a tantrum—no dirt roof against them now, which means they're outside the tunnel. Snow crunches under her toes, but her shoulders won't budge. She has time to think the bear will bite into her hands first, then her skull, when the bear's body jams against the jab stick with a force that collapses her arm, while in the same movement, the body she can no longer control suddenly shrinks away from the tunnel walls and the flesh of her face scrapes the floor: someone is pulling her by the ankles out into the snow—Ronelle. The breath goes out of her again as the bear's claws dig in—the sow on her back—and then Eva's weightless, gasping. Ronelle shouts. Eva, rolling to one side, can see a blur of fur, flying snow, cracking branches.

The bear charges at Dawna, Dawna who has run to the top of a rise and stands beneath an oak tree with her jaw clenched, a tiny woman in a maroon polyester coat, eyes popping from her pale face, each hand waving a stick. She faces the bear. She grimaces and growls. The bear hesitates. Shakes her head. Perhaps the sow finally feels the effects of the jab stick. Ronelle, advancing from behind, aims the dart gun and gets off a shot. The bear turns, runs a few yards toward Ronelle—herky-jerky, like a character in a Charlie Chaplin film—before she falls over.

For a moment, everyone's frozen, Dawna on the slope with the sticks still ready, Ronelle with her hand holding the dart gun, Eva collapsed in the snow, grateful for the steam in front of her face, moist air that indicates breathing.

"*Damn.*" Dawna runs down the slope and and kneels next to Eva. "Are you alive?"

Ronelle arrives, runs her hands up and down Eva's back. "She tore up your coat, but I don't see any blood."

Dawna nods toward Ronelle. "Good shot."

Ronelle straightens up. "*You* didn't even give."

"Daddy used to say, *Hold your ground.* But I never had to do it before. Not for a bear. Wait'll Bobby hears. Holy Jesus."

The two women regard each other without rancor. Eva wants to applaud.

"What happened?" Ronelle asks Eva. "You get stuck?"

Eva nods. She's in new territory, pulled there by her ankles, her body no longer insisting its way toward or away from a thing she can't control. The pain in her back has subsided, though her scraped nose throbs. "That was insane."

Ronelle rubs her back. "We're okay." She looks at Dawna. "Right?"

Dawna nods.

"We're mountain women." Ronelle offers Eva a hand.

"Can you get up?"

Eva waves her away. "I will."

"Clock's ticking. You want us to get started?" Ronelle takes a step toward Dawna.

Eva doesn't answer. She rolls over, bends her knees, puts her hands under her head and looks up through the branches. A nuthatch hops up and down the ridged trunk of a tree, making muted beeps. Afternoon light slants through the trees. Above them, turkey vultures circle; steadily, the creek trickles. The snow numbs Eva's back, and when she closes her eyes, she feels the ground supporting her body, molding itself around tree roots, offering its dark, porous cavities to all that dwells beneath. She hears Ronelle saying, "Look, we took it this far. Let's finish up." When Eva opens her eyes again, Dawna's legs are disappearing into the tunnel.

Nearby, Bear B45 is inert, paralyzed by the drug, incapable of harm. Eva needs to tend to her while Dawna and Ronelle deal with the cubs. She ought to put drops in the sow's unblinking eyes—it's the humane thing to do. And then there are the measurements to take, the blood to draw—but right now, she doesn't give a hoot about the data. Something's bubbling inside her, making her giggly and light, loosening her muscles. Her hair's come down. It floats across her shoulders. She tests herself. Wiggles her fingers. Bends her knees. With Mama bear down, Eva's coming to life.

Dawna reappears, emerging from the den with a sack of squirming cubs. She and Ronelle will tattoo the cubs' lips, weigh and measure, as they've been trained to do. They'll gather the data, pack up their things, return the cubs to the den, and make sure the sow comes out of her stupor. After that, they'll jostle out the unplowed byway and disperse in darkness on the usual road. Eva's father will call with the inevitable news about her mother, but now on the mountain, in the afternoon light, Eva gets up to tend to the sow. One hand on the warm body, she feels the bear's ribs rise and fall with each breath. She reaches for the eye drops, squeezes the dropper's bulb to release liquid into the staring darkness of a wild thing's eyes. Prepares the syringe and vials, parting the fur to take the bear's blood. The team has come this far—despite everything. Yet the numbers are merely numbers. Heart rate. Height. Weight. Percentages of this or that vegetation. Her team is recording things that are or have been. They're completing the necessary work.

PLEASE USE THE PASSWORD

U nder her straw hat, Evelyn broke off the brown seed
-heads and dead stalks winter had left, then heard the answering machine pick up inside her house. She'd programmed
it so Kitty Wells' maple syrup voice melodically invited the
caller to *please use the password, just say the words of love.* Evelyn rested her weight on her palms, like an infant in a crawl,
as she heard the Radiologist's voice.

"This is Dr. Sawyer?" the voice said girlishly. "Evelyn Mc-
Nair can give me a call at—"

"Want me to get that for you?" Barry yelled out through
the screen.

"No."

"It's the doctor!"

"That's okay!"

"But it could be—"

"I'll call her back later!"

Barry came out the door in his bare feet, walking gingerly over the gravel, coffee mug in hand. He squatted beside her and pulled out a weed. "Is there something you aren't tellin' me?"

"Everything doesn't have to be told."

"I'm gettin' a lot of *no's* today."

Earlier that morning, she'd refused his offer to put his own voice on her answering machine.

"You don't live here," she'd said, reaching into her kitchen cabinet for a coffee mug, then shutting it closed just-so, "but thank you."

"Just trying to protect you from the crazies." Raising his thick gray eyebrows, he'd retreated a step, shuffling on his bad leg, and held his calloused palms between them as if to fend her off.

"That's how it all starts." She cinched the belt of her flannel robe around her thickening waist. The robe still smelled of their mutual sweat, and she was naked beneath it—a sight she herself did not like, but Barry had said he appreciated a younger woman. She was 60 to his 62. He called her honeyrumped and sweetfaced, and whenever she mentioned a part she didn't like (the sagging skin under her arms or the blue veins in her thighs), he'd roll up her sleeve or her pants leg and start kissing her there. With his dimples, a person wouldn't think he'd once carried an M-60 through the jungle, except that he still did his boot camp push-ups. About the rest, he preferred not to speak.

"How *what* starts?"

She'd folded her arms, sent him a glare. "*It.*"

He'd lifted his own coffee mug between them, sipping, but did not appear discouraged. When she sat down at the table next to him and spread out the newspaper, she allowed him to touch her fingers lightly, then squeeze, before she reclaimed her hand to turn the page.

Crouched among the dead stalks now, she avoided looking at him.

"I don't think you need to know everything. I don't even think you want to."

"Oh I want to," he said.

She'd felt the lump in her breast a few weeks ago, checking herself in the shower as she did on the first of each month. Her mother had had a bout with breast cancer, though in the end she'd died from a heart attack, so Evelyn knew to be careful, and she got herself to the doctor right away. There had been one indeterminate but worrisome mammogram, and this was the second. She hadn't mentioned either to Barry, nor to her grown son, Bart, nor even to her women friends. Why worry people if there was nothing to worry about?

Inside her cotton sweatshirt now, she could feel the fabric against the two nipples she still had. On the other side of the board fence, as if nothing disastrous was happening to Evelyn, her friend and neighbor Joan, a college professor one year from retirement who lived with three Siamese cats, discussed politics.

"I *love* Hillary," Joan said, in what Evelyn knew to be her phone voice. "They say she's a heartless bitch, but what's she supposed to do? If she was any more emotional, they'd say she was a bubblehead."

Whatever *else* was going on for Hillary Clinton in the presidential primaries, she at least appeared to have two excellent breasts, as did Evelyn, despite the reality of gravity—though now, a sagging breast seemed far better than none at all, and none at all better than *death*—especially now that she'd finally, after years of dreaming and mooning over country-western music, gathered enough money to retire and move into cow-boy country in central Washington, far from the bleak hog-raising flatlands of Minnesota; yes, she was in the great State of Washington, where she was closer to the drama of mountains and rivers, the plenty of vineyards and orchards, as well as the fruit of her womb, Bart.

In the yard, Barry touched her fingers, apparently un-bothered by the dirt under the nails, grimed into the skin. "I want to know all about you. Every inch."

"You got enough to worry about."

He raised his eyebrows. "Like what?"

"Getting the hay in."

"Not today. Today I rest."

"Well, I'm operating on a need-to-know basis."

"That's okay." He broke off some brown stalks, dug down with a screwdriver, trying to get all the root of a bindweed, but she could tell he was hurt. "I've been there before." He tight-ened his lips. "Can't say I like it, though."

"I'll be right back." She went into the house, turned on the answering machine, and played back the message. Dr. Sawyer wanted her to call back.

She dialed the number. When Evelyn explained herself, the receptionist said, "Oh, I'm sorry, but the doctor will have to talk to you herself. She's in surgery right now. What time can she reach you?"

Evelyn had never, after a mammogram, had to wait for a doctor's call. She knew it was bad. She sat down at the kitchen table, holding her head in her hands. Her cat, Loretta, twined about her ankles.

It was as if that morning's dream had been some kind of warning. "He was right *there*," she'd said to Barry when she'd awakened to the vibrations of the cat's purr penetrating the blankets between them. In her dream, Bart stood next to the bed trying to say something, but Evelyn hadn't been able to hear him above Barry's snoring.

"A course." Barry had tried to pull Evelyn closer. Evelyn didn't give. She didn't want to dislodge poor Loretta, who'd lost an eye but miraculously survived her encounter with something she'd run into (coyote or dog), not long after Evelyn had moved in.

"It was the same feeling I had right before the tornado—" Evelyn began.

"You say that flag across the way just kept flyin?"

"It did."

"While everything else—"

"Wrecked. The wind blew so hard they found a piece of straw embedded in a tree trunk. That's not in the dream, now, you know. That's the truth."

"Piece a straw?"

She pointed a finger off to the side. "Like it was an arrow."

"Shrapnel."

"Guess you saw your share of that."

He stiffened, as usual, evading the reference to his the time in Nam. "You were saying about the feeling—'"

"Without that tornado, I'd still be ignorant." It was a complicated story, but she'd explained to him that fifteen years ago, the tornado that had taken the roof of her house in Owatonna, Minnesota, had also revealed receipts and telephone records that had given away her husband's numerous infidelities. "I was taught to trust people," she'd explained. "So it came as a pretty good shock." She snuggled closer to Barry. "Maybe that's what disasters do. They wake us up. Without it, I'd still be playing the fool. But as for the *dream*—"

"Well then I'm gonna call it the perfect storm." Barry had kissed her so deeply she'd forgotten about the cat and moved her elbow, sending Loretta off the bed with a yowl.

Now at the kitchen table, phone silent beside her, Loretta on her lap, she heard the screen door open. Barry's bare feet padded across the carpet. She felt his hands on her back.

"There'll be daffodils any minute," he said.

"I hope I'm here to see them," she said.

Barry sat down beside her. "You better tell me what's goin' on."

She shook her head.

What if the Radiologist called and she didn't answer it? Then she'd never find out the results. Would it be like the tree falling in the forest—if there was nobody there to hear about a malignant lump, could it still do harm?

If she didn't get the news, she wouldn't have to break it to Barry or her son Bart, who worried about everything anyway, but lately of course had more than enough with his wife Shirley stationed in Baghdad. Everyday Bart looked at a website that could tell you exactly how many new dead and wounded American soldiers there were. Not too many, Evelyn thought, compared to over a million Iraqi deaths blamed on the US invasion, but none of *those* was the mother of her grandchild.

"You shouldn't be looking at this stuff," Evelyn had told Bart last time she was there, setting Iris on his lap to distract him from the computer. "It doesn't help Shirley."

Poor Bart, old enough now to have the hair thinning on top of his head, had taken up his daughter and held onto her the way he used to do with the yellow blanket she remembered his father taking away from him when he was six years old. "I need to keep the whole truth in my mind."

"Why?"

He shrugged. "Part of living. Part of knowing I'm alive."

"The living are as true as the dead."

"I'm aware of that, Evelyn."

She'd gotten used to it she guessed, but still hated the fact that he didn't call her Mom. He'd started using her first name right after she'd left his father. She still remembered Bart with those braces on his teeth saying it was *far better*, as he put it, *to see your parents as individuals than as the inhabitants of roles*. The inhabitants of roles. Like a role was a little burrow and they were moles blindly making their way down the tunnels. About the same time as he started calling her Evelyn, he also began to write poetry and listen to music she thought was downright ghoulish. She blamed his girlfriend, Marly South-ard, though she was grateful, too, that Marly'd been so wild she couldn't stick with one guy, so Bart had finally let his hair go from the Mohawk and curl around his ears, and then he'd found Shirley, who seemed to Evelyn a good, faithful woman despite the fact that she'd ventured thousands of miles away, but that—of course—wasn't *her* choice.

On the radio just then, the song went to Merle Haggard. Barry made a face, but didn't ask her to change the channel. He was a rock 'n roll fan, Led Zeppelin among his favorites. Not Evelyn. When she was younger, with her curly dark hair and eyebrows against her pale (and some said sweet-featured) face, people who knew country music often said Evelyn looked like Kitty Wells. Barry didn't know "It Wasn't God Who Made Honky Tonk Angels" until she put the earbuds on him and played him the song. He'd nodded politely but eyed with suspicion the life-sized stand-up cardboard Clint Black by her entryway. "You sure you don't want to hold out for a cowboy? We got plenty of em around."

She *had* intended on a cowboy when she moved West, but when they'd sat on the folding chairs where she'd met him, at the Red Cross waiting to donate blood, she'd moved into easy conversation with the big-shouldered easygoing dimpled man who'd given up his morning because he had the blood type of a universal donor, and pretty soon she'd forgotten all about the cowboy idea and given Barry her phone number.

Much later, at his house, she'd asked, "What if you wake up in the night thinking I'm the enemy and let me have it?" She'd pointed to the unloaded rifle next to his bed, ammo in the drawer of the bedside table.

"What if *you* wake up mad thinking I'm your ex-husband and cut off my dick with a butcher knife?" At her house, he'd pointed to the pepper spray in her dresser drawer and the carving knives in the kitchen.

It was hard enough to trust a man when you were sixty years old with two healthy breasts, but with one going south, maybe she should just be calling it off.

"Don't you have someplace you have to be?" she asked Barry, who was sipping his coffee carefully, as if waiting for her to speak.

"Are you tryin' to get rid a me? 'Cause if you are, I'm happy to go."

"What do I really know about you, anyway?"

He shook his head as if to clear it. "Huh?"

"You don't tell me diddly-squat."

"You know enough."

"I know you grew up here and inherited a hay operation. I know about a few women you've been with in town. But I don't know a thing about what you did in the war."

She knew she was treading on dangerous ground, but it was better than thinking about her own mortality.

Her neighbor and friend Joan had said she didn't see how Evelyn could trust a guy if she didn't know whether he'd killed boys younger than Bart, children Iris's age, mothers like Shirley. If he wasn't going to explain what had happened in Vietnam, all that was left for her were images of bloodied heads on stakes from *Apocalypse Now* or magazine cover images of women and children's bodies thrown into ditches during the

My Lai massacre. Of course, she'd argued with Joan, it was equally possible she was kissing someone who'd soiled his pants and run the other way in combat and couldn't shoot a can if it was six feet tall, or much better, kept his body between the villagers at My Lai and harm. "My ex-husband was a conscientious objector, and look what kind of a partner *he* was," she'd said.

"What's past is past," Barry said.

"I wish what was present was past," she said.

"I don't know how to help if I don't know what it is." He rubbed her shoulders. "What can I do you for?" he joked.

She thought of him faithfully riding the tractor in the hay field, using the rake to turn the mown green blades to *even-out the dryin*, then returning a couple days later, depending on the weather, with the baler. She liked it that he was a native Westerner. The Kittitas Valley was famous for timothy hay, which was shipped to Japan, the country that had had some of the worst of war, but where today Barry's hay was fed to dairy cows who turned it into butterfat while—the sound of a small plane flying overhead made her think of it—new bombs were dropped on Iraq.

How must people down here look to the pilot—mere dots inside the neighborhood's maze of board fences on top of what once had been a big, flat hayfield? The horizon to the north was dominated by the Stuart Range—she'd learned the names of the mountains when she dreamed over maps in Minnesota. They were snow-covered, toothed, magnificent as the Grand Tetons. A mile to the west, buildings clustered in the small town of Ellensburg, where wine tastings had become as common as beer swilling, and university professors drank coffee next to cowboys.

She raised her chin, watching the sky out the window. If some machine was up there taking infrared photographs, would the lump in her breast be visible? If cancerous, would it be growing and dividing even as he watched? So close to her chest cavity, maybe it would look like a mutated heart. One that was immune to the password Kitty Wells sang about—one that grew on bad genes and fear instead of love.

"Maybe it's lunch time," she said to Barry.

She got up to wash her hands, then made them each a turkey sandwich, his with mustard and her own with mayonnaise. In silence, she chewed each bite, savoring the tart dill of the pickle. She wiped her mouth and washed the dishes before she looked at the telephone again.

You lived your life, you thought love was seeing only the good in people, but when the sirens went off, you had to expect a big blow. She'd been home with Bart, thank God, and got into the basement in time when the twister hit Owatonna, but they could hear it—a sound just like they said, something like a train engine—and after that, Bart, always a worried kid, withdrew even more. They'd had him to specialists, counselors. He'd got into drugs for a while. He wasn't good at holding a job. But now he was a damn good father, though of course he had Iris to the doctor when the little girl so much as sneezed. Still, he was there with the child day after day. Not running around with other women as his father had been. He sang lullabies to the little girl that Evelyn had sung to him. She'd even caught herself humming one to Barry the other night.

"Sweetness," he'd murmured in his half-sleep. "That takes out the sting."

"See here," Barry said, looking into his water glass now. "About Vietnam. It's best we just leave that alone."

"How do you know if you don't say anything—you know, get it out, it won't turn"—with cancer on her mind, the word came naturally—"malignant?"

"A person has to find his own way. This is mine." He pushed his plate away, took a long swallow of water.

"Tell me one thing," she said. "And then I'll tell you my

story."

He looked around the room, as if trapped. He sighed. He stood up. "Let's walk."

They went out the front door into the neighborhood of new houses in which Evelyn lived. They passed a couple teenagers shooting a basketball into a hoop that had been placed on the curb by the side of the road. It was a nice day, and several of her neighbors were out walking their dogs. Evelyn and Barry waved to them. They turned onto a gravel bike path that had once been a railroad bed, and after a few minutes, finally, they were alone.

Barry cleared his throat. "I'll just say it: I was in 1/9."

"1/9?"

"First battalion, Ninth Marines. Later known as the Walking Dead."

"The Walking Dead?"

"We had the honor of the most casualties ever, in the entire history of the Marine Corps. We did a lot of ops, but 2 July '67 was the worst. Outnumbered six to one. I think I told you I carried the M-60. The M-60 is a big machine gun, one of our baddest weapons. I always kicked ass and took names." He stumbled a little.

"Meaning—?"

"Kill." His voice was soft. "That's what it means." He spoke louder, as if defending himself. "Kill before you or your buddies are killed." He cleared his throat.

They were walking beside a marshy field, with a profusion of cattails. Red-winged blackbirds trilled. Evelyn imagined how the field would look strewn with dead soldiers, Barry holding the gun that had done them in. It seemed impossible, so she focused on the birds again. Once the firing stopped, would the birds return?

"We lost so many, I—" He pointed to the ground in front of them. "They'd be right there in front a you. The guy you'd just talked to. Shot in the head. And the guy next to him, and the one next to him." Barry pointed, then stepped away from her a foot and pointed at the ground again. I didn't know how I was still alive. Still don't." He blinked hard. "I was just a kid, and—"

Evelyn put a hand on his arm, but he didn't respond, so she let it fall.

"It was—like when you get into a hornets' nest and just run. You don't even think about it. That's what I did. They popped me in the leg," he touched his sore knee, "sometime. I'm not sure when. I—I—," he dropped his chin to his chest. "I never shoulda made it. Many days I wished I hadn't."

"I'm glad you did."

"Whoever survived lived because we ran and we hid. And they came looking for us. I saw them shoot guys, point blank, in the head. When our guys showed up to get us, I guess I was outta my mind. I don't know what I said or did. It didn't matter. I felt like I was already dead. They took me out a combat then. Made me what we called a REMF."

"REMF?"

"Rear Echelon Mother Fucker. Typewriter duty. A fucking Remington Raider." His face wore an expression she had never seen—eyes narrowed, upper lip curled, if he were looking at something disgusting.

"Rear Echelon Mother Fucker means you're alive," Evelyn said.

He shrugged. "You could call it that."

She shook her head. "I can't imagine it. I don't know how you can function as well as you do."

"You do what you gotta do," he said. "Not a day goes by I don't think about it. Part a why I don't talk about it. It's right here, all the time." He put his hand on his heart, then touched it to his forehead.

Evelyn tried to take his other hand, but he wouldn't hold

on.

"I'd rather not have told you any of this. It's just ugly. That's all it is."

She looked down the trail at the wide sky, the green of the fields stretching out on the edges of the new suburbs.

"I probably have breast cancer," she said. "I don't know how far it's spread, but I'm sure that's what the doctor is calling me about."

"Jesus, Evelyn."

"Compared to what you've been though, it's not much. I didn't want to bother you with it."

"Well." He reached for her hand, and she let him have it. "We're a pair."

"The Walking Dead," she said.

"Not you," he said.

"You don't know that."

They walked back to the house in silence, holding hands. When they passed the boys at the basketball hoop, she said, "You weren't much older than that."

He shrugged, tried to withdraw his hand, but she wouldn't let him go. Inside, she made tea, put the mug before him, and kissed his cheek. "I guess I'll get this phone call over with."

She asked him to go in the other room so she could be alone while she talked to the doctor. He nodded, avoiding her gaze.

After she got through the call waiting, the receptionist and the nurse, Dr. McNair's voice came onto the line, "We'll have to go in and see," the doctor said, meaning cut into Evelyn, look inside the breast tissue, maybe remove the breast entirely. "We don't know how far it's spread til we're in there."

Evelyn closed her eyes. She heard the buzz of a small plane again. The wind had not yet started to blow, so later, she could turn the water on the lawn, set the timer, move it around til the wind came up again. A bee had come in, causing Loretta, lying in a sunny spot on the rug, to raise her head, watching with her one eye while her tail twitched, before she jumped into Evelyn's lap. She imagined Barry humming "Stairway to Heaven" while he sat next to her in a folding chair at the hospital holding her hand. She knew *him*, not the soldier. She knew the man he was now would let them jab a needle into his vein if she needed the kind of blood he had.

She went into the next room, where Barry waited at the kitchen table. When he saw her in the doorway, he got up and put his arms around her. She let herself slump into his chest.

"Guess I don't have to ask what you found out," he said. "Even the cat's upset." Loretta was twining around their ankles meowing as if in distress.

"You didn't sign up for this," Evelyn said.

"If you want me to be here, there's not a wind big enough to blow me away."

"It'll be a rough ride."

He squeezed her hand. "I'll be a cowboy."

THE OPENING

When the phone rang, I ran into the laundry room, where the old brown rotary model hung. It was a totem of misfortune from my first marriage—the final straw being Chuck's call from the police station after his second DUI. This was a different kind of call.

"Diane, it's me."

"Kay?"

"It's me," Kay said again. "I've hit a deer."

"What?" I said, not because I didn't hear her, but because I didn't understand. How could she hit a deer next door? After three years of friendship, I knew her routines: she was usually in her studio between 8 am and noon, not answering the telephone or allowing interruptions. Me, I was nothing but interruptible. If it wasn't my daughter Chloe who needed me, it was my second husband Tom, the volunteers at the animal shelter I managed, or the peace group that had become more active since George W. Bush had squared off with Iraq.

Listening to static and a brief delay after Kay identified herself—this told me she was on her cell. "I hit a deer," she said again. I looked at the canned goods lined up on the basement shelves, suppressing an urge to move a jar of applesauce that had somehow invaded the green beans.

"On Payback Mountain Road, " Kay said. "The deer is hurt. I think it's hurt badly."

"What about you?"

"I think I'm okay."

"You *think*?"

"Shaken up."

"What about the car?"

"It still runs."

"Why are you out there?"

Payback Mountain was only a few miles out of town, but we'd had some snow and then a covering of ice that hadn't yet melted—beautiful, encasing the living stems and branches of trees in ways I'd been trying to paint when Kay called. It had been hard won, that basement studio space and the few hours for myself on Saturday morning. It had involved tears, a yard sale, a rearrangement of Chloe's visitation schedule with her father, and an expenditure of money I didn't have for art supplies.

"This deer," she said, "it's not dead. You're the Humane Society. I thought you'd know what to do."

I imagined Kay standing over the deer—a waif-ish woman with dark hair gelled and spiked like a teenager's. Red stone in one nostril, a garnet—her favorite, she'll tell you, because it's the color of violence. Big-eyed and pert-nosed, she looks like a college kid until you get up close, and then you notice the fine lines around her mouth and her eyes, the shallow crease between her eyebrows. Her hair, her figure, and her big dark-lashed eyes made her look much younger than I did—we were both fifty-three, but I was an ordinary fifty-three, with the swaybacked look of a woman who's had a child, belly and thighs softening, dark hair with streaks of gray.

"Look, are you okay?" I asked Kay again.

"Just a little whiplash."

"Do you have a blanket or something?" I asked.

"No." She paused. "I don't know what to do."

"Stay warm," I said. "I'll be right there."

I bundled up—neck scarf, gloves, coat—wishing I'd at least had time for a coffee. I didn't want to wake Tom: if we were lucky, the problem would get up and run off before I got there. Later I wondered if I'd derailed myself on purpose. Rescuing Kay was distracting, but there was an immediate result, unlike the long, uncertain process of making paintings.

I left a note on the kitchen table: *Went to see Kay. Be back for coffee.*

As the defroster blasted the windshield, I looked through the ice at Kay's house next door—vintage 1940s, a saltbox with long narrow windows and a covered front porch. She'd painted the house blue with cranberry trim. The stained glass front door and odd metal sculptures in the yard suggested this was the home of an artist, whereas I had an ordinary front porch with a dog leash coiled by two pairs of Chloe's boots.

The light still burned over Kay's front door, and her truck had left tire tracks in the snow-covered driveway. Her soon-to-be-ex-husband Philip had given Kay the house and the four-wheel-drive while he'd taken the older Honda Civic—odd, but he knew Kay cared more about capacity than efficiency: she needed the truck to carry her photographic equipment, and despite his transgressions, he was the type to take care of her as best he could, the big sap, even as he departed with a young graduate student who worked in his lab.

Since he'd left, Kay had called me for help more and more. I tried to say things to help Kay feel better—what an asshole Philip was, how much he'd lost, how she might be better off. I'd been divorced when Chloe was just two years old. I knew how it felt.

"Call me anytime of the night or day," I told her. And she did. Tom didn't complain. I'd say he was a saint, but he was a sound sleeper. She didn't call when it was convenient for me, because then she herself was working. Nor would she answer the phone when she was painting or developing photographs. Which is why, when I called *her* one day, frantic because I'd locked Chloe out, and she'd be coming home from her sixth grade class before I could get home from work, and I couldn't reach Tom, Kay couldn't help me, either. Chloe had tried knocking on Kay's door, but when Kay was working, she didn't answer. I had to leave work early. When I got home, I found Chloe sitting miserably on the front porch, shivering in the cold.

I drove out of the neighborhood and along the edge of the college campus. Shades were still drawn in the red brick dorms with their white-pillared porches. Generally I loved mornings, and I loved the quiet, but today neither gave me the usual feeling. Nor did Crockett's downtown, with its bricked-in square and striped awnings over the tidy shops. Instead irritation prickled my eyes.

I drove past the post office, where we'd had a demonstration a week before against the impending Iraq War, with three hundred people marching around the post office in the pouring rain. Not as many as you get in a day patronizing Wal-Mart but not bad at all for a town the size of Crockett, far in the southwest of Virginia. I'd been an anti-war activist during the Vietnam era, too, because my friend Collin, the first artist I'd ever known, was drafted and didn't make it home.

After that, I went to college on an Art scholarship but got pregnant and then married to Chuck, my first husband, after which I spent most of my time taking care of Chloe and trying to pretend Chuck didn't have a drinking problem. I told myself it was better to keep the family together than to deprive Chloe of a live-in daddy or give up Chuck's salary to make my own way as an artist. Painting was one thing as a hobby, another thing entirely if I had to use it to feed my kid.

I followed the road out of town, past the university's dairy barn full of big-eyed Jersey cows with deer-colored hides, their udders ballooning. In a neighboring pasture, a couple of mares and foals ran back and forth along a fence as a pickup approached to feed them. Once in a great while, when Chloe was an infant who'd sleep in her stroller, and I was still married to Chuck, I'd set myself up in a lawn chair by that fence, with my paints. Just now, over the pasture, toward the mountains, a soft pink light filtered through the clouds. I berated myself for abandoning my easel.

On Payback Mountain, I drove a mile or two, then followed the road's hairpin curves onto the ridge until I saw Kay's car off the shoulder.

I parked behind her red Ranger with its motor running. Kay stepped out of her truck, wearing jeans and a green sweatshirt.

She gestured toward her purple coat, spread on top of the doe which lay panting, its head and neck upright over straight front legs. The deer sat on her haunches, one leg stretched out behind her, a bone piercing her skin. She was partly in the road, partly on the road's shoulder.

"We should put out some flares," I said to Kay, "just in case." Then I turned back to the deer. Her snout was bloodied, her eyes glazed. When I approached and touched her neck, she didn't flinch. She was panting. Just last week, I'd seen a dog brought into the Humane Society in shock like that. I'd called the vet to euthanize it.

Animals. The true innocents. They broke your heart. So many things happened to them that they didn't deserve. I touched the doe again, wanting to communicate something like compassion. The doe panted a little harder, and I felt sick. I turned to Kay.

"What were you doing out here anyway?"

She lifted the camera around her neck, as if in answer.

"This time of morning?"

She nodded toward the sky. "I liked the light."

"So what happened? You couldn't see her?"

"I was looking toward the sun." She gestured toward the East, where the sun was rising higher. "Then before I turned my head back to the road, there she was."

"You couldn't have missed her?"

She nodded toward the drop-off on the other side of the road. "I wasn't taking any chances on this ice." That was when I thought to look at her truck. The grille was smashed, the windshield cracked, the fender dented in. "Listen, I'm glad you're all right," I said.

In truth, I was touched by Kay's concern for the deer. It was unlike her—if I'd had to bet on it, I'd have bet she'd leave the deer. Maybe I'd misjudged her.

I considered whether we might slide the blanket under the doe's body and lift her into the back of Kay's truck. She probably weighed as much as the average woman. But why would we? The Humane Society could barely pay its vet bills—

I knew no one who'd set the leg for free. Beyond that, there might be internal injuries, and even if there weren't, and the leg was fixed, what kind of life could such a deer live? It was not exactly a backyard pet. The deer was done for.

Sun glittered from the ice and snow, the harsh light intensifying the pounding in my head.

"I need to think about this," I told Kay.

Kay nodded and opened the door of her pickup—to stay warm, I thought, but instead she pulled out the camera and unscrewed her lens, replacing it with a bigger one. Then she focused on a nearby post, the pickup's dented fender, the blood spattered on the road. She moved slowly, considering the ground like a detective looking for clues: tire marks, tufts of fur.

I went back to my car, opened the hatch. The Humane Society wasn't like the pound—we didn't euthanize as a matter of course. We had to call a vet. I carried no supplies for lethal injections, but from my toolbox, I picked up my dad's old hunting knife, touched my finger to the blade. Still very sharp. As a girl, when I'd wanted to be a veterinarian, my father had encouraged me to watch him butcher a deer he'd shot. "If you really want to help animals," he'd said, "you've got to learn how they're made."

Watching a beautiful deer turn into ground venison and roasts convinced me I'd rather be almost anything but a vet—I didn't really enjoy the *insides* of animals—yet after my father died suddenly in a car accident a few years ago, and my mother started getting rid of his things, I went through every tool he had, looking for that knife.

Kay was back in her truck, sitting in the driver's seat behind me, warming herself. I held the knife between my body and the deer, out of her vision. I didn't want to talk about what I had to do—I might lose my nerve. I returned to the doe, my back to Kay. The doe's breathing was labored, and crystals of snow clung to her coat. She hadn't changed her position. I held the crown of her head against my belly. Still in shock, she offered no resistance.

In front of me, the road went only a short distance before it disappeared down the other side of the ridge. A driver going that direction might think she was going to plummet. The sun rose at my back, and beyond the disappearing road, between the leafless, gray-barked trees, a distant, dark mountain turned from black to blue. My fingers stung. The deer shivered. I squeezed my eyes shut.

"What do you think?" Kay called from behind me. "Can we lift her into my truck?"

I didn't answer. I cupped my left palm under the doe's chin, lifted her snout, felt for her throat's hollow. I held the tip of the knife against her neck. I'd have to cut her carotid artery, then use the serrated edge to open the wound. The cut had to be deep, fast, accurate. I focused my attention—as if the doe's neck were only an unwieldy fabric or a thick mat. To make the right cut required precision, concentration. Later I would compare the motion of the knife to a violinist's bow cutting deeply into the strings, but it wasn't like that, not at all. It created no music. The act was not an act of making.

When the doe fell away from me, I stepped back, sick to my stomach, fingers still tight around the knife handle. What had been warm and alive, though suffering under my hands, had once pushed itself from the womb, risen on new legs, danced out into the world to graze on new leaves. The doe may have mated, had fawns, and watched its offspring leap across the road into the woods before she made her last crossing.

I heard something click behind me. Kay's shutter. Moving toward me, camera banging at her chest, Kay skidded on the ice, then caught herself, went down on one knee to steady herself, and focused toward my face. Click. Then toward the doe. Click, click.

The ground felt atilt, light glaring from the ice. I put my hand in front of my face as she aimed at it. "Please."

The doe's neck opened, raw, red, like a mouth. Kay's shutter clicked as she moved around the body. It entered my mind that she might have planned all this—she'd expected I'd have to kill the deer and wanted to get it on film. Had she hit the deer on purpose?

"This isn't a sideshow," I said.

"Can you hold the knife up?" she asked. Her face had the bland, interested expression of someone watching a ballet.

My throat tightened. I wanted to push her into the snowbank, yank the camera from her neck, throw it off the ridge. Instead, I turned away, cleaned the knife in snow, and replaced it in the tool box.

"Please? It's an opportunity," Kay said.

"Is that why you called me out here? To give you something to shoot?"

She shrugged, eyes wide. "This is what I *do*."

I slammed the car door and made a U-turn, skidding back onto the road.

Tom and the dog met me at the door. Tom was still in his checked pajamas, his eyes magnified behind his thick-lensed glasses, his feet in wool socks. He'd charmed me early on in socks like that, skating across the wood floor of his house toward his piano, where he sat and played ragtime before he grilled up our hamburgers. "What happened?"

"Kay hit a deer up on Payback Mountain Road." I told him the whole story.

Tom poured coffee from the carafe into my favorite mug, the one with a picture of Chloe when she was a baby, as I sank onto a kitchen stool. When I got to the part about slitting the doe's throat, Tom rubbed the bald spot on top of his head.

"How'd you even know how to do that?"

I thought of my father sitting in his armchair reading *Sports Afield*, light reflecting from his glasses. "It's a long story."

The phone rang. I picked it up automatically.

"Diane, I—" When I heard Kay's voice, I hung up.

"I take it that wasn't a sales call." He came around behind me and put his hands on my shoulders, as if to begin a massage, but I stiffened. "No?" he asked.

"I'm not getting into that," I said.

"Into what?"

"Every time you massage me, we wind up in bed." I stood up, letting his hands fall from my back. "I've got other things to do. No more Diane the Submissive. No more Ms. Nice Guy, no more Ms. Enabler. I've got to go. I'll be in the basement. I don't want to talk to anybody, not even Chloe, unless it's an emergency."

I passed the paint shelves, the canned goods, the stack of empty boxes. I turned the corner at the room I'd transformed into my studio, where there was a window that let in some light. It fell on my unfinished image, and the image compelled me to pick up the brush I'd left. The wooden handle felt warm, then warmer, as I painted. I filled in the sky. I made a trunk and more branches and twigs, but then, disappearing into the work, I abandoned form and let the colors talk.

It was a month before I spoke to Kay again. I'd stopped by the university's student center, and to get there, I had to pass through a public art space where Kay, as I discovered, was having an exhibition. It was called "Blind Curve." I moved through the press of celebrants holding their glasses of punch to see images of the doe I'd killed.

In Kay's photographs, trees glittered with ice in the pink

dawn, and the patterns of blood and fur were oddly beautiful. The doe herself, alive and injured, looked dignified instead of suffering and in shock, and the photographs of her cut throat had been enlarged, so the flesh was not flesh but something abstract, the wound a ragged seam of cells as benign as a pomegranate. I scanned the photographs, afraid I'd see myself in the act of killing, though I also half-hoped she'd captured the painful reality, offering some kind of meaning in the sacrifice, but I saw only my hands, enlarged artificially so they appeared surreal, the morning light and objects sharp-edged with ice and snow.

As I stood there looking, Kay herself appeared through a door at the back of the room. "Well hi there, stranger."

She looked thinner than she had a month ago, the skin swelling beneath her eyes outlined in black. Her close-fitting red dress showed her stockinged legs and creamy breasts. She arranged her glittering scarf and held steady on her high heels.

"Are you finally going to talk to me?"

"Congratulations," I said.

"You don't mean it."

I looked at the floor. "Does it matter?"

Briefly I met her eyes, but then she avoided my gaze, and her jaw tightened. "This is my *opening*," she whispered.

"Is that a *real* deer?" I heard an elderly woman ask her balding companion as she pointed at the carcass in the photographs.

SWIMMERS

Dorothy Coover, resident biologist, was driving a Fish and Wildlife Service Jeep to the Necropsy Lab when she passed the building where the animals were sacrificed and saw all the cooperative education students sitting in the back of a green truck, their rubber boots up to their knees and their heads bowed. Her lover Lenny Moore, the tall young man from Virginia, stood in the pick-up bed, his back against the cab of the truck, clasping his hands in front of him as if he were about to be led to the gas chamber himself. Dorothy swung left, pulling her Jeep next to the truck, and said, "What's going on?"

The students looked up. There were five in all—Lenny, who had been assigned to Roger Harkin, the raptor man; Sharla, a sweet little blonde from University of Maryland, Dorothy's own charge; and three from Endangered Species whose names Dorothy couldn't recall.

Lenny swung down from the pick-up bed and put his hands on the passenger door of Dorothy's Jeep. He bent like a willow. His hair, the color of tree bark in shadow, fell forward over his shoulders, and he smiled, revealing what Dorothy felt were endearingly crooked teeth. Lenny glanced at his watch, then spoke back over his shoulder. "They're finished." He seemed to be in charge.

One of the other young men—Bob? Bruce? whoever he was, he was dark, dressed in cut-offs and a tank top, his arms and chest muscular and furred—jumped down from the truck, turned the wheel on the carbon monoxide tank to shut it off, and opened the door of the shed. Inside were crates of mallards, all of them dead. The girls hopped out of the truck now, too, to load the crates into the pick-up. In their shorts and halter-tops, attire Dorothy and the other biologists allowed because of the heat, they looked like they were ready for a stroll on an oceanfront boardwalk. Only the rubber boots, footwear for pens layered in duck shit, gave them away. Dorothy herself was more modestly dressed—knee-length shorts, sleeveless blouse. She rubbed one hand up and down over the opposite arm. It was firm, because she worked out, lifting weights at home and then, every morning, jogging along the path by the river that cut through the research center, fighting what would otherwise be a natural decline. Her husband Tom, on the other hand, had let himself go.

"With a little effort, you could have your old body back," she'd told him.

He'd smiled, opened the jar of peanuts he was holding, shaken some into his open palm and tossed them into his mouth. Then lifted his shirt and slapped his big gut joyfully.

Lenny, like the other cooperative education students,

wore cut-offs and a tank top, revealing a dark, even tan and the long musculature of a swimmer. He even made love like a swimmer, thrusting with a steady rhythm. They used the cot upstairs in Dorothy's building after hours. Last time—in fact, last night—the yellow light of dusk had come in through the Venetian blinds, stippling the room as if she and Lenny *were* underwater. Dorothy wasn't much of a swimmer, though with Lenny she had felt she could learn.

But it was August. Only a few days left before Lenny returned to college. The co-op students worked six months on jobs in their fields, then went to school for six months. Lenny was 23, a senior; this was his last co-op stint. Dorothy was 37. Tom, a statistician, worked across the research center—two locked gates and numerous animal pens between him and his wife.

She'd visualized the scene of Tom's outrage, had panicky periods when every ring of the phone made her want to confess, sure one of her lovers would call, a la "Fatal Attraction"— a movie she was sorry she'd ever seen—to tell Tom what had happened, to ruin her life. And there had been medical scares. The time she'd thought she was pregnant, she wouldn't have known with whose baby; the time she'd finally—after the second lover—had an AIDS test. Normally it was hard, when she was in the first throes of passion, for her not to despise Tom. There were things about him that were so . . . to put it kindly, unattractive. For instance, he had a habit of sniffing, when he was concentrating hard, that made her want to scream. A way of putting his hands on her shoulders when they were at parties that felt like *ownership*. And there were little things he shouldn't be asked to change—clipping his toenails into the sink, crumpling his towel over the bathroom rack, leaving a fine film of bath powder over everything . . . it was idiotic that such things should bother her . . . and his sense of humor, though it had been one of his prime attractions for her, was sometimes inappropriate. After the breast lump had been found, for instance, but before the biopsy, he'd tried to cheer her by talking about how she'd look as a Picasso: cut-up. Fortunately the lump was benign, but it had further convinced her that it was important to be living, by which she meant not missing chances, such as the chance she had with Lenny.

She'd noticed him last year among the new crop of co-ops partly because he was tall and lean but also because unlike the other students, he didn't act shy around the biologists.

"It's hard to believe the kid's 22," Roger-the-Raptor-Man, as the co-op students called him, had said last year. "He's incredibly savvy."

This year Roger had lent Lenny to Dorothy one day when both her co-ops were ill. The two of them worked quietly taking blood samples, Lenny pinning each duck to the metal table and holding its wing while Dorothy worked the needle.

Afterwards, as they were washing up, Lenny said, "You're impressive."

"Why?"

"You're not squeamish. I've seen some of the others mutilate the veins because they were afraid they'd hurt the animal."

Dorothy shrugged. "I guess you get over that. You have to."

Lenny stood in the lab watching her dry her hands. The lab was in a building next to the duck pens. From there it was a long walk to the offices on the other side of a locked gate. Lenny and Dorothy were alone. When she turned away from the sink, she could see that he admired her. But, she told herself, he was the student, she was the supervisor; it could mean her job.

Later, though, it occurred to her that he was *Roger's* student. She wasn't his *direct* supervisor at all. They passed each other on the Center's roads at least once a day. Leaning out of their open Jeeps, they slapped each other's palms and laughed.

Sometimes stopped, engines idling, to chat. Eventually met for lunch. Then walks after work. The first time they made love, it was in the woods. On a bed of moss, he pulled off her pants. She helped, giggling. Then lay back. He stroked the long, soft hair between her legs, then moved it aside to use his tongue. She looked up at the sky through the pines and said, as if speaking to God, "Thank you."

The feeling of gratitude stayed with her, convincing her—oddly enough—that Lenny was helping her to love Tom more. She was able to come home, after a night with Lenny, and kiss Tom with real affection. She imagined herself like the doves in the Songbird House allowed to fly free while the students cleaned their cages. It wasn't much trouble getting the doves to come back; they returned on their own, feeling safer in their cages.

But now Lenny indicated the truck and the crew, so recently sitting in the bed of the pick-up. "We just wanted to have a moment of silence for the ducks." He shrugged his shoulders. "We all know this has to be done, but we have our feelings about it. I wouldn't want you to think we were slacking off."

She tried to read his face. Was he saying this for the benefit of the others? Surely he didn't really worry about her judgment of his work. Nevertheless, the way Lenny was looking at her, his eyes full of compassion for the animals, Dorothy was touched. She licked her lips and swallowed. She fingered her hair, felt it frizzing in the humid heat, and was sorry. She, too, liked the ducks. Their friendly faces. Their beautiful heads, especially the males with those sleek green feathers. She didn't like to sacrifice them, but she and other biologists at the Maryland station were feeding small amounts of oil to the mallards. They wanted to know the effects of oil spills so they could help the mallards' wild cousins. To judge the effects, they had to

look at the internal organs. "It's no problem," she told Lenny.
"It's only natural to feel sorry."

Last night, when they'd been in the room with the cot,
he'd said she was the first woman he'd ever really loved.

"We're so happy together," he'd said, as if he were arguing.
"So *right*."

"Yes," she'd said. Then, waving her hand to indicate the
cot, the room, the building. "But these are only experimental
conditions. What would happen to us in the wild?"

If there were predators," he'd said, nuzzling her breasts,
"I'd protect you."

She leaned down, cupping his testicles in her hands. "Bird
eggs," she'd said. "Delicate and beautiful as bird eggs. If we
were wild birds, we'd probably step on something precious in
the nest."

Lenny pulled her up by one arm, roughly, so that she
pushed his hand away and said, "Ouch." He pinned her to the
bed, holding her shoulders, his hair grazing her face. "Bad
things can happen in captivity, too." When he let go, he turned
away, curling protectively, knees to his chest.

Trying to make him feel better, she'd suggested they meet
for weekend trysts after he went back to school. But he was
young, she'd reminded him. She didn't want their involvement
to mean he might miss finding someone with whom he could
spend his life. "Eventually you'll have to give me up," Dorothy
had said, and tried to smile, though the idea was grim.

When she had got home from her evening with Lenny, she
had slipped into bed next to Tom. The ceiling fan's blades cut
the air, uh-wmm, uh-wmm. She laced her fingers across her
chest. Tom wriggled deeper into his pillow. Although he was
turned away from her, she could see the familiar curve of one
ear. She was no longer amazed that he couldn't tell when she'd

been with another man. Years ago, it had enraged her—especially with her first lover. She'd felt Tom slipping away from her then, spending more and more of his energy on his dissertation, and she guessed his withdrawal fed her sense that she *deserved* to do what she was doing, that she had a right to it.

Thinking about her first affair now, she couldn't believe she had fallen for the sleepy-eyed musician who had played his guitar by a pond on the edge of campus. The songs were sweet and sad. Now she couldn't remember any of the words—only the feeling of longing, the music tugging at her viscera. She was, after all, only an animal like the ducks with their slippery intestines, their sleek brown livers. After a few sessions, Russ asked to read her palm. He took her hand and said, "I knew it. See all these lines? It means you're an old soul." The come-on seemed ridiculous to her now. But when he kissed her hand, his mustache tickling, he broke some barrier of space. They embraced for awhile, then walked to his van. He drove onto a secluded road and pulled over. She was frightened. When they actually made love, she couldn't relax, and it was slightly painful. Afterwards, though, Russ stroked her hair, kissed her forehead, and massaged her feet. He was married, too. He said the first time he tried to sleep with another woman, he couldn't.

"Her name was Dorothy, too," he said. "I've never forgotten her. You're like my second chance."

She got home late, but Tom was still at the library. She imagined him in his cubicle reading about standard deviations, glad to note that she could see the irony in this, that her sense of humor was intact. She took a shower and washed away the smell of Russ. Then she lay naked on the bed and thought of Russ's fingers in her hair and his body over hers and the feel of him moving inside her. It was like falling from a cliff.

In the morning, she found Tom sleeping soundly beside her. Nothing was different. She got up and made coffee. Tom came into the kitchen, sliced a bagel, and put it in the toaster.

"Get a lot done last night?" she asked.

"Not enough, goddamnit." He rubbed his hand over his face. "I have to go right back to it this morning."

She hugged him, but he pushed her gently aside and said, "Coffee."

Eventually, of course, Tom had finished his PhD and they'd both got the jobs at the research center two states away. She and Russ said good-bye. Good-bye was, they agreed, built into the contract, as it was with John, her second lover, whom she met a year later and who, after a few months, drifted away.

Extramarital sex was, she thought now, lifting her hands up to the air that was pushed down over her body by the fan blades, a kind of drug. The air felt good. She threw off the sheets. Tom stirred and flung an arm across her stomach.

"You smell clean," he mumbled.

She'd taken a shower after she and Lenny made love. The shower was next to the cot in her building, in a room meant for biologists whose experiments had to be tended through the night.

"I took a shower," she said.

He touched the calf of her leg with the ball of his foot. "Um."

She put the flat of her hand on Tom's naked chest. She'd massaged Lenny's chest earlier, tracing the line of dark hair from his belly to his groin, then lightly stroking his penis until she took it into her mouth. Now she moved her hand down between Tom's legs. There had been nights when she'd made love to Tom after she'd been with Lenny. Lenny made her feel beautiful, passionate. She'd slide into bed next to Tom and massage him, kissing his neck, his chest, then get on top. She'd lift her breasts, stroke her nipples with her fingers.

But now, depressed by Lenny's impending departure, she let her hand fall away. Tom turned over. She curled into his back, comforted by his big, inert body.

She could not yet smell the ducks, but soon, in this heat, she would. They would take the animals to the Necropsy Lab. The students would pluck them. She and Roger would remove the livers, examine and weigh them. When they shouted out weights, the students would record them, one sheet for each animal, identifying them by the tags on their webbed orange feet.

Sharla was crying as she loaded the crates. Lenny looked at her, then at his hands, then back at Dorothy, stricken.

"I'm sorry it has to be done," Dorothy said.

Lenny came toward Dorothy with a crate in his arms; the green head of a mallard emerged, its beak hanging open.

None of the co-op students would look her in the eye.

"I'll meet you at the lab," she said to the group of them, to Lenny, although he didn't look up. She put the Jeep in gear and drove down the lane. Early morning steam rose from the road, and trees arched overhead, closing out the sky with their branches. Only 9 a.m., but already it was an effort to breathe. When she scratched her cheek, oil from her skin caked beneath her fingernails. At least the Necropsy Lab would be air-conditioned. The Jeep roared. With the pedal to the floor, it only did 35 mph. Through the open sides she could see the forest, viney and tangled, whizzing by; if she'd been here earlier, no doubt she'd have seen deer. There were several thousand acres in the refuge. There was more than one small herd of deer, occasional foxes, beavers, otters. Even, once, a bobcat. But in this heat the animals were probably already bedded down, possibly unconscious. It was the only way to escape.

The road divided, and suddenly, where she should have gone left, she found herself, without planning to, veering right, taking a detour by the eagle pens. Across from the eagle pens the resident behaviorist had built an observation tower. In the top was room enough for two to sit shoulder to shoulder, watching through binoculars and taking notes. Lenny had spent hours there, documenting the birds' nesting rituals on his own time. She'd been there with him once or twice.

It was common for the co-op students to become attached to a particular species. Sharla, for instance, was trying to raise Louisiana heron chicks which otherwise would be killed. Biologists from the Gulf sent Dorothy the heron eggs. She put them in the incubator, coating them with a drop of oil every day. When, despite the oil, they hatched, she had no use for the heron chicks—nor, she had argued with Sharla—any way to raise them. But she had agreed to let Sharla get an old heat lamp out of a shed and set up a cage for six of them. Sharla had to feed them from an eye-dropper five times a day, at least. Dorothy didn't think the chicks would live, but she always tried to give the co-op students the opportunity to find things out for themselves. She could understand Sharla's horror at the manner in which the chicks were dispatched: in a sealed jar with a wad of cotton coated in chloroform. To demonstrate to Sharla that she understood what was involved in killing them, Dorothy had accompanied her to the incubator room for the first slaughter this year. In the palm of Dorothy's hand, each day-old chick had trembled, warm and utterly vulnerable. It wasn't as if, despite her years of experience, Dorothy didn't feel anything when she put each chick into the jar, sealed the lid, and—eyes averted—felt it thumping the sides of the jar trying to get out. And then, to take the little bodies to the incinerator and toss them in, as if they were no more than offal, as if they hadn't—just now—lived. It wasn't as if it didn't affect her.

She turned off the Jeep and listened to the eagles calling back and forth. She climbed into the observation tower. How did things look to Lenny from here? What was it like to live in his young, strong body? To believe, as he'd told her he did when he watched the eagles mate, in true love? Though the air in the tower was stiflingly close, and her skin was already coated with perspiration, Dorothy watched the birds. The female sat on the nest, her wings slightly outspread, looking ragged. The male flew to the floor of the pen, picked up a dead rat, and flew back to the perch, tearing off meat. Still clutching part of the rat in his claw (Dorothy could see the white tail looping over the perch), he hopped toward the female, bent his head to hers and fed her some meat. It was too bad for the rat, but the birds were magnificent.

Roger-the-Raptor-Man who was, despite the air-conditioning, heavily perspiring, had already begun the dissections in the Necropsy Lab. Lenny was assisting. They wore white lab coats over their clothes. Dorothy had come in through the door from the hallway. The other co-op students sat on the loading dock out back—Dorothy could see them through the back door—plucking the birds' breasts.

"Ah, Dorothy," Roger said, wiggling his eyebrows. "This isn't Oz." He looked up from the duck he was cutting, holding his gloved hands up like a surgeon's. The birds were laid out on shiny metal tables, lights shining onto the open cavities of their breasts. Roger's round glasses caught the light, and he wore a comical expression. Lenny kept his back turned, but she glanced at the naked backs of his legs emerging from beneath the lab coat.

She put on her rubber gloves and lab coat, then brushed her bangs out of her face. Her hair was cut short in a kind of bob, the back of her neck shaved. She stood in front of the air conditioner for a moment, letting it cool her, picked up a scalpel and approached the metal table, coming up next to Lenny. His hair hung on either side of his face; she couldn't read his expression. She adjusted the lamp so that it shone more directly onto the bird's plucked breast. Roger had already moved to the other table and called Sharla in to assist him, leaving Lenny with Dorothy.

Dorothy sliced open the bird and peeled the flesh back from the breastbone, revealing the organs. The bird was still warm. She located the liver, removed it deftly, and put it onto the scale. She read out the weight. Lenny glanced at the bird's leg band, recorded the number, then placed the carcass into a garbage bag. Eventually it, like the heron chicks, would go into the incinerator.

The loading dock out back was heaped with birds. In this group, there were 250. There would be three other groups, for a total of 1,000 birds. It was important, Roger and she had agreed—and Tom, as statistician, had concurred—to have a decent sample size.

"What a waste," Lenny muttered, putting another carcass into the bag.

Dorothy clenched her teeth and cut into another bird. The more quickly they could get this over with, the better for all of them. Didn't Lenny think she had feelings, too, about this? Did he really think she enjoyed the stink of dead birds, her hands in their open cavities, their still-warm livers sliding around in her fingers? It was hardly appetizing . . . yet she kept glancing at Lenny's legs, the swell of his hips beneath the lab coat. Even when she willed herself to focus on the work, her body was aware of his, as if her cells had become magnetized and Lenny's held the opposite charge. She kept shifting away from him, sighing deeply to release her frustration, then yawning as animals sometimes, she knew, did when they saw a thing they wanted but couldn't have. It was called *displacement behavior*.

You are so beautiful, she kept saying, silently, to Lenny. His thick, slightly waved, dark hair; his big long-fingered hands; his dark, smooth skin—skin, she had told him, like an Indian's, smooth from his throat to his hairless chest to his bellybutton, where the black line of fur began. His eyes were the surprise:

a blue so pale they were almost gray. They gave him an eerie look that Dorothy found exciting. But now he stood beside her, the shoulder-length hair still shielding his face, his body turned away from hers, resisting.

And why shouldn't he? She had had to remind him of their circumstances. Of what was real. Of what he'd known all along. Certain limitations.

For a while they worked in relative silence, Roger or Dorothy calling out an occasional weight, Sharla or Lenny saying, "Okay," or "Got it." The air conditioner, an old model, roared. Dorothy, standing in front of it, had goose bumps.

Then Roger called out a weight, and Sharla said in a strangled voice, "Oh, no. It's number 34." She turned away from the table, stripped off her rubber gloves and threw them into the plastic garbage bag by Roger's table. Tears streamed down her face. "I'm sorry," she said, and ran out the door that led to the hallway.

"What's the problem?" Roger asked, his hands in mid-air.

Lenny looked at Dorothy then, for the first time since she'd come in, and in his look was a world of blame. "She loved that bird," he said.

Roger said in an accusing voice, "She knew it had to go."

Lenny shook his head, drawing his lids down over his fierce eyes—blink, blink—like the eagle's. Then he, too, drew off the rubber gloves and cast them into the garbage sack. "I'll see what I can do for her."

The other co-op students went on plucking; they hadn't heard. But Roger opened the back door. "Buddy?" That was the dark, muscular student's name—not Bruce or Bob. "Buddy? We need you in here."

Buddy got up from the loading dock, dropping his plucked bird into the pile. "Where'd everybody go?" he asked, glancing in through the door.

Roger shook his head. "It's hard to sacrifice these birds,"

he said to the other students. "Especially if you get attached to one. But we've got to get these livers out while the birds are fresh. If you're going to have feelings about it, try to have them later, okay?" He looked at the two remaining students, two girls from Endangered Species—both in shorts and halter tops, one slim, the other heavy, both of them brunette. He glanced at Dorothy. "Which one do you want?"

The smell of ducks decaying rapidly in the heat wafted in through the door—a sour, overwhelming stench. Dorothy's stomach heaved; she tasted bile. Heat came into the door in waves. The laboratory appeared to be moving. Both of the women looked impossibly young. One of them opened her mouth like a fledgling's. What were their names—Melanie? Melinda?

"You all right, Dot?" Roger took her under one elbow.

She closed her eyes.

"Shut the door," Roger said to Buddy. "Help me get her to a chair."

The two of them supported Dorothy, leading her to a metal folding chair. Roger told her to put her head between her legs.

The other co-op students came in, too. She could see their legs surrounding her, then heard another door open and close and saw the legs of Lenny and Sharla approaching as they returned; Lenny's voice asking, "What's going on?" Roger's hand on her shoulder. Then Lenny's, briefly cool on the back of her neck.

"Do you want me to call Tom?" Roger asked.

The tiles on the floor were smeared with blood, and Dorothy's bloody gloves were still on her hands. She stripped them off, then put her hands to her forehead. One of the girls from Endangered Species bent, retrieved the gloves, and tossed them into the garbage.

"I'll call your husband," Roger said.

She gripped Roger's hand, still on her shoulder, and shook her head. She raised herself up, sitting straight, and looked at Lenny. He seemed to be at a great height, but he bent his knees and came down to her level. She felt a ripping sensation inside her chest.

"Breathe," Lenny said.

Roger's hand disappeared from her shoulder, but the co-op students still surrounded her, forming a protective circle. Lenny leaned his forehead into hers. She wanted to speak, to say she was sorry, she loved him, she couldn't give him up, but it was as if a great hand were forcing the words back down her throat.

Sharla said, "I think she's trying to talk."

But Lenny touched his fingertips to Dorothy's lips. "Shhh. Shhh." He glanced at the other students. His fingers were cool on Dorothy's bare shoulders as he stood up. Leaning her forehead into his belly, she felt her heart fling itself against her ribs.

"What's wrong with her?" Sharla asked.

"It's too damn hot in here," Roger said. "I'm surprised we're not all fainting."

Lenny said, "She just needs to regulate her body temperature. Being out in this heat, then coming back in—the conditions changed too fast." He moved behind Dorothy, rubbing her back, then cupping his hands at the base of her neck. "Just relax."

She leaned back, letting him hold her head, chin upraised as if she were floating. When she opened her eyes, she saw Lenny's face outlined against the white ceiling, as if he were already a phantom. She wanted to reach for him, but her arms, as in a dream, were too heavy to lift, and already he seemed far away, like a life raft at the top of a swell on the horizon.

THE LOOKOUT

For the first time in our five years of marriage, my husband Jim and I had agreed that I would spend several weeks of that summer on my own, driving to Colorado to drop my son Shane with his father, my ex-husband, then camping out of my small truck, rigged with its miniature camper shell. Although Jim was invited and had tried going west with me before, he couldn't really relax on those trips. He needed his rituals, his showers, his cappuccino maker.

We were in bed when we made our decision. It was a Saturday morning in the Spring, blustery weather finally giving way to daffodils and cherry blossoms. A golden light slanted in through the venetian blinds, illuminating the deep reds of our cherry furniture, the plush recliner on Jim's side of the room. On my side, the night table was cluttered with books, magazines, colorful stones and feathers. Jim, with his back to me, was looking at an attractively framed Victorian print of a boatman ferrying a woman down a Venetian canal. The woman trailed the fingers of one hand in the water and held a ruffled umbrella over her head with the other. Jim yawned, stretched, and turned toward me. "Why don't we go to Europe this year? Do something different while Shane's with his dad."

I stiffened. "What if something happens to Shane? It would take forever to get from Europe to Colorado."

Jim rolled over, put an arm across my belly and moved closer. "He'll be okay with his dad, won't he?"

"I don't know."

"I'm sick of the Rocky Mountains," he said. "I need more culture in my life."

"We live in Washington, DC. What more do you want?"

"Art. Cafes. A different language. Different kinds of people—"

"We've got all that here. What we don't have is open space. Solitude." I turned over and raised up on one elbow. "Jim, I admit. I'm an addict. I need my Western fix."

"Fine. Go ahead."

He lay on his back, elbows jutting, hands laced under his head. The silhouette of his nose, broken in a car accident, gave him the look of an Irish middleweight, though he was the least athletic man I'd ever known. He smelled of soap and wore soft cotton, freshly laundered pajamas.

He rolled toward me again, kissed me lightly, pushed a warm hand under my sweatpants so it rested on my bare hip. "Go on out there. I can go to Europe by myself."

"Are you serious?"

"Why not? We're grown-ups. We have a commitment. But we don't have to share everything."

I turned on the light so I could see his face. The white spot showed at the hump of his nose, a sign that he was serious. "Are you trying to tell me you want out of this marriage?"

"No." He touched my face. "Jesus Christ, no. I just don't want one of us to chop off an arm or a leg so we can fit together."

Later that summer, driving further West after I left Shane at his father's house in Colorado, the conversation came back to me. I missed Jim, but I didn't miss having to line up an expensive motel with a clean shower every night for him. I loved building my own campfires, my mind empty except for their flames. Yet there were long nights, too, when, alone in my sleeping bag, I wondered whether Jim's refusal to come along meant he really didn't love me. Whether my insistence on going West meant I really didn't love him.

I traveled from Utah up into Idaho, west to Boise, then north to a little resort town named McCall, where on the map I'd seen the Payette National Forest dotted with high lakes. I liked to fish, but that day I was hiking just for the view. As the trail steepened, it turned to granite. Small rock cairns marked the way. Not only was a blue lake visible below, but further away still, I could see a long narrow valley with the Payette River meandering through. Huge clouds built over the valley to the south, some perfectly white, others with dark undersides, flashing distant lightning. As I rounded a final curve, the lookout tower appeared.

A staircase zig-zagged to the floor of a catwalk, surrounding the square tower. In the roof, there was a small chimney like the type to vent a woodstove. As I made the final pitch toward the summit, gradually I came to see even further: to the west rose the Seven Devils Mountains, jagged peaks including a wilderness area that I knew plunged into Hell's Canyon, where the Snake River separated Idaho and Oregon. From the ridge where I stood, something about the peaks, in all their youth—rocks not yet worn smooth like the Appalachian range closer to home—moved me to tears, and I stood on the edge of the summit, weeping. In part this was grief for the loss of the life I had lived in Colorado with my ex-husband Gary. There were times when I missed that life and missed Gary, who had shared my passion for views like these. Gary had been the one who'd wanted out of the marriage, saying he felt suffocated by domesticity. In the end, he'd literally disappeared into the woods, coming home only as long as he needed to replenish his supplies or take an occasional shower. Finally I'd moved east to be closer to Shane's grandparents, people I knew would be glad to spend time with him. I'd met Jim after a couple of years—a man who didn't need wilderness and therefore, I'd thought, wouldn't wander.

The breeze faltered, and a cloud passed over the sun: the still air brought out the mosquitoes. I slapped them on my bare arms, as if slapping away my grief and self-pity. I was smashing one on my cheek and brushing away the blood when a man came up over the rise. The aluminum frame of his backpack jutted above his head, making him look even taller than he was—he was tall, all right, over six feet. His brown hair grew over his ears, but it was neatly combed, and he had a full beard in which there were shades of copper. He wore jeans and a T-shirt over his thin body. I think it was his boniness that kept me from feeling threatened—that and his way of maintaining distance between us, as if he were aware that a woman alone on a mountaintop with a strange man might need some room to move away.

"Hi there," he said. Then, glancing at the blood on my cheek and the look on my face, no doubt, of someone who'd been crying, he said, "You okay?"

"Oh." I brushed at my cheek. "Just slapping mosquitoes."

"They can be fierce up here."

"You come up a lot?"

He pointed to the tower at the top of the rise. "I'm the lookout. Charlie."

"Janet."

He said he'd just come back from town, where he'd had a shower and picked up supplies.

I glanced at the darkening sky. "I wonder if I ought to get down before that storm hits."

"Typically they start in the south and move east to those ridges over there." He pointed. "They've been skirting this area ever since I've been up here."

"Not much action for you then?"

He shook his head. "You want to see the tower?"

The stairs were almost as steep as the steps on a ladder. Where they reached the catwalk, a square hole had been cut. We lifted our bodies through. Then we were on the balcony with sweeping 360 degree panoramas.

He pointed out the peaks and valleys, naming them. Together we watched the sky. We were quiet, but it was comfortable, a silence the place seemed to request. I liked his careful manner. I liked the fact that he read—not grocery store novels but good literature—he said he liked Tim O'Brien, Robert Stone. The Stone novel he'd read was "incomprehensible in parts," he said. "Just like his movies."

"You like reading about war?"

"From here I can tolerate it." He looked out at all the space around us. "From here I can tolerate just about anything."

"I imagine."

"Want to see the rest?" He gestured toward the glass enclosure.

A bunk rested in one corner, the sleeping bag pulled up, clothes neatly folded on top. A low counter was affixed to one wall. There was a clean pot in the sink. Another clean pot had been placed on the burner of a small propane stove. Next to the stove were two big containers of water. It was primitive, all right—I had already noted the privy below, a long walk in the middle of the night, I'd thought.

A circular podium covered with a map dominated the exact center of the room. "What's that?"

"Fire finder." We stood looking at the map with its latitudes and longitudes marked. "It doesn't really find the fires. I do that." A voice blared out of the radio clipped to his pocket. He turned it off. "I've got a bottle of Jack Daniels." He rubbed his eyes, then looked at me in a way you look at something you want.

The bourbon made me dull, it's true, but I'm not blaming the alcohol. I made my decision the minute I let Charlie know I was married, and he said, "There are no rules up here." Even so, it took a few hours before we moved our stools close together, thigh against thigh, and he put his hand in my hair. Eventually I unbuttoned his shirt. His long torso was bony, but he smelled of wood smoke. I moved my palms across his chest, his belly. He kissed me deeper, harder. I took his hand and led him to the cot. He sat on the edge, hesitating, but I kissed him again and then pushed him down. I slid his pants off and saw that he was ready. Then I was on top of him. The lightning, by now, was closer in, all around us, sometimes so bright I could clearly see Charlie's face, eyes closed, mouth working with pleasure. I bit his shoulders, licked his throat, pressing my tongue into his mouth and moving on top of him until his fingers dug into my back and he jerked hard into me. Afterwards, I nestled into the crook of his arm on the narrow bunk, listening to the thunder move down the valley.

I slept. But sometime during the night, when I reached for the man I thought was Jim, I was surprised awake by the bony feel of him. I tried curling into his back as I would Jim's, but Charlie's sharp spine repelled me. When I tried turning away from him, I found the bunk was too narrow.

My stomach began to lurch. I tasted bile. I got up once, thinking I would be sick, pacing around the small room. I imagined grabbing my pack and running down the trail in the dark, returning to the familiar truck. I imagined this was all a dream from which I would wake up, but then I looked at Charlie's form in the bed and wrapped my arms around my naked body and remembered the feel of his mouth on my breasts, the stickiness from our lovemaking still between my thighs.

By morning I was dressed, sitting by the window. When Charlie woke up, he asked, "You okay?" His hair was flat on one side of his head, his eyes cloudy from fatigue. The blanket still covered his lower half, but I was struck again by the sheer length of his torso. Jim was a much smaller man—a man in miniature, I often thought privately.

"I'm not feeling too good." I stared at something solid, the window ledge, something neutral that wouldn't bring back the previous night's passion. "My stomach hurts."

He sat on the edge of the bunk, now, penis tucked between his thighs, holding his head. "Hell. We should've drunk some water after we had all that bourbon."

He pulled on his pants, then filled one of his pots with water and put it on the stove. It was early morning, the sun's rim just showing over the peaks. The tower was filled with a gray light. He went out the door and stood on the catwalk until the water boiled. The sun rose higher, and the sky was a deep blue. He handed me a cup of tea. "You're not regretting it, are you?"

"It's not you. You were great." I waved my hand toward the view. "I liked the way we shared all this."

"Past tense?"

I looked into my mug. "I'm thinking about my husband. I've been a faithful wife both times, until now."

He pulled a stool close to mine. "You haven't done anybody any harm."

"I'm not so sure."

As we sipped our tea, the sun rose higher until the tower was illuminated with yellow light. Charlie went outside onto the catwalk again. He looked out over the empty mountains into the cloudless sky. I could see the ligaments in his neck relax. I could see his entire body unclench.

I gathered my things, then waited for him to come inside and say goodbye. I made up his cot, smoothing the blankets so they looked as they had when I first entered his tower. Still Charlie stood there, his profile as natural a part of the sky as the spire of any spruce tree on the mountain. Finally I went outside and touched his back, but he didn't move.

"Aren't you even going to say goodbye?"

"Goodbye," he said. Half turning, he nodded, then resumed his position. So I walked down the stairs and away from the tower. I walked down the trail, then stopped and looked back. He still didn't turn around.

Hiking down the trail, I didn't see the lake or the flowers; didn't notice—as I had on the way up—the way the aspen leaves shuddered in the wind, catching the light. When I got to my little truck, it didn't comfort me the way it usually did, waiting there like a faithful dog. My stomach still hurt. My mouth tasted stale, and my arms and legs ached.

As I drove back down the mountain, then south toward Boise, where I'd turn east again and head for Colorado, then home, I thought again of the way Charlie had touched me. I said to myself, *You let that man enter you. You let him into your most private space. Jim's space.* I turned it over in my mind until I convinced myself that somehow, Jim had figured it out. From his room in Paris, he'd felt it. And when I imagined this, I had to know if it was true. So I stopped at a pay phone. When Jim answered, he sounded tired. I listened hard for the sound of a woman in the background. "It's midnight here," he said, "but I'm glad you called. I wanted to tell you I had café au lait where the Lost Generation used to hang out—you know, Hemingway and Fitzgerald and all those guys. I got you a postcard. You can show your students."

"The Lost Generation. Wow." I stood on the rickety porch of the Mountain View General Store, next to the newspaper dispensers. To the north, lightning slashed down toward the Payette mountains. Had it ignited a fire, maybe in Charlie's jurisdiction? Jim's tone sounded the same as always. He didn't know anything, not at all. I imagined him in his clean cotton pajamas breathing sleepily into the phone. His room would be tidy—shoes polished and lined up, suits pressed and hanging, T-shirts neatly folded in the drawer. He'd be smelling clean, as usual. Maybe it would be a different kind of clean, though, with those European soaps.

"All those writers," I said. "Hanging out in Paris. Sleeping with each other, sleeping with the locals. Getting into fights. Marrying, divorcing. I don't know. I bet there are a lot of unwritten stories."

"Um-hmm."

"Sounds great," I said. "The stuff of imagination. Sitting where they sat. Thinking about their lives."

"Like I said, I thought of you here."

"I'm thinking of you here as well."

"You okay?' Jim asked.

The storm clouds came closer, thunder rolling toward me across the valley. "You hear that?"

"No."

"Thunder. I should probably get off the line."

"But you're okay, right?"

"Yeah. It's just—McCall wasn't what I expected."

"What'd you expect?"

"Something a little less wild."

"I thought you liked wild."

"I don't know." I looked toward a distant ranch house,

where the yellow lights came on as the sky darkened. It was probably dinnertime. They'd be sitting together around a table of steaming food—husband, wife, children.

As I continued down Highway 95 toward Boise, the sky moved like a series of veils tossed into the wind. The fabric to the west was clear, cloudless, the slanting light of dusk turning it purple. To the east, high anvil-shaped clouds gathered, some gray, others pure white. To the south, toward the desert, a half-rainbow arched across a newly washed sky. But to the north where I had come from, in the rearview mirror I could see gray-black fingers connecting the sky to the earth, and I could see spectacular lightning.

All across the high desert of Idaho, east along the Snake River under the relentless sun of midsummer, I imagined the worst: I was on the birth control pill, but I would get pregnant or get AIDS; or I would be all right physically, but the experience would form a wedge between Jim and me whose origin Jim would never understand; or Charlie would find me somehow and confront Jim; or Shane would find out and hate me. As the sun lowered and the air cooled, the light slanting from among the clouds softened the harsh angular buttes and jumbled lava rocks. The speed limit was 75. I went 85 or 90 through Idaho, then Wyoming, until I reached the Colorado border and made camp. By flashlight there, I wrote about Charlie in my journal, then tore out the pages and threw them into the fire. The smoke from the paper, damp from my spilled coffee, was thick and unpleasant.

In Colorado, Shane burst from the door of his father's house to meet my car. He looked wonderful—tan, blonde and fit from his time in the outdoors, the muscles in his arms hard from paddling. He looked older than his twelve years, I thought. When I hugged him, I had the feeling there was ground under my feet again, ground I hadn't quite realized was missing.

Gary waved to me from the doorway of his house, a 1920s white clapboard with a deep front porch in a neighborhood of similar boxy working class houses. His kayaks were hung on one side of the house; he'd parked his battered van, with its racks for the boats, in the weedy driveway.

"Have a good trip?" he asked as I came up the sidewalk with Shane. His blonde beard needed trimming, I noticed, and his fingernails were still bitten to the quick. His legs protruded from beneath the fringes of his cut-offs. His legs were long and bony, I noticed, not unlike Charlie's.

When we reached the Virginia border, Shane and I began singing a made-up song—"We're almost home"—in screeching, tuneless voices. We exited from the Beltway and followed the Potomac River for a while before we entered our quiet neighborhood of two-story brick houses with gleaming windows. I was struck again, as I am everytime I return to the east from the small towns of the Rockies, how much money Easterners—including Jim and me—spend on their houses. No RVs parked in these driveways. No kayaks here. Not a shred of unwatered grass browning under high altitude sun. No views of the snow-capped mountains, either. There was instead a feeling of luxurious comfort and of safety. We could see nothing from here that was not manmade, even our carefully landscaped yards.

In the house, I collapsed on the rug in front of the cold fireplace, belly down. Jim straddled my back to rub my shoulders while Shane pounded up the stairs to see what Jim had put there, a gift from Paris, he'd said.

"That feels great," I said as he worked the kinks out of my shoulders. "Your touch is magical." By then I couldn't even remember Charlie's. I could barely recall the sound of his voice, the expression in his eyes. I had only a vague memory of the shape of him, the angular feel of his arms. The surprising difference between his kisses and Jim's, Charlie's mouth so much smaller, his lips thin.

Jim said, "I really missed you."

"Me too."

He leaned down to kiss me, then slid his hands under my blouse to touch my breasts. "I missed this, too."

"No buxom Parisienne girls?" I said.

"No. No well-endowed cowboys?"

"No." I kept my face turned away from him.

A few weeks later, we went to a faculty party in the home of Gil Thorpe, an art professor who had a passion for the French countryside. Jim kept pointing out rural scenes in the paintings on Gil's walls, delighted because he recognized the places. Overwhelmed, finally, by Jim's enthusiasm for the pastoral, I escaped to the back patio. I was sipping my chardonnay, watching the late-afternoon light over the rooftops of the other townhouses, when I overheard Jim talking with Gil through the open window.

"No," Jim was saying a bit sadly. "She had to be out West with her son."

"Well, next time give me a call," Gil said. "I'm in Paris every summer."

"You know who else you might run into?" Jim asked. "Leslie Payne." His tone was warm. I missed a few sentences as a colleague greeted me, then caught, "Right, she's in Languages."

I knew Leslie—not well—only enough to recognize her. She was not unattractive, but for my taste she was too well-packaged: her hair streaked blonde, her nails painted, her legs always stockinged, her feet in heels. Probably she was the type, though, to enjoy museums and tidy foreign countrysides. Jim hadn't told me about seeing her.

We drove home along a parkway that felt like a tunnel—trees arching over the roadside, their leaves forming thick barriers of deep green. Afternoon thunderstorms had kept everything wet and growing. Outside the car window, the humidity hung in sheets. My head felt heavy, my mouth dry from too much wine. I dropped my head into my hands, pressing my fingertips against my eyelids. I imagined Jim across the table from Leslie in a sidewalk café, reaching across the table to touch her hand.

"Did I hear you saying you saw Leslie Payne in France?" I lifted my head to look at him.

"I told you about that, didn't I?"

"No."

"Oh. I thought I had." He drove steadily, guiding the car around curves that made my stomach lurch.

"What happened with you two?" I asked.

He frowned, the white spot showing at the hump of his nose. "How much wine did you have?"

We rode in silence, the tension between us thick, until I said, "I need to know, Jim."

"Nothing happened, all right?" He punched on the radio, and for a time we listened to the placid voices on National Public Radio. Finally he turned the radio off. "Don't you trust me anymore?"

When we got home, I drew a bath, then slid into the hot water, letting it work into my neck. I'd had enough wine, it was true, but I wasn't drunk. This was a different kind of ugliness. I looked at my naked body. It was mine to do with as I pleased, mine to share with whomever I chose. And Jim's—a body I knew almost as well with its moles and freckles, scars, patches of hair and pockets of loose flesh—Jim's was his. As were all his experiences and memories.

I stayed in the tub until the water grew tepid and my skin pruned. Finally Jim knocked on the door to see if I was all right.

"Come on in," I said.

He stood in the doorway.

"I'm sorry. It was the wine talking."

"Okay."

"Let's forget it ever happened." I got out of the tub. Jim took a towel from the rack and patted my face, then wrapped the towel around my body and held me.

"I had an affair." I spoke into his shoulder. "Out West. It was just one night. I got—I don't know—"

Jim released me. His eyes narrowed and his mouth worked. "Why?"

"Something about the place."

"The *place*?"

"It was a lookout tower."

"Did you fuck a tower or a guy?" His tone was sarcastic.

"I'm sorry. It just happened."

"It just *happened*?"

"That's wrong." I tightened my towel under my arms. "I made it happen."

"What do you want me to say?"

"I wanted everything clear."

"It's clear, all right." He shook his head, turned, and walked out of the bathroom. I could hear his feet on the carpeted stairs. I was shivering. The drain still sucked at water swirling down in the tub, a few of my long dark hairs riding the whirlpools. By the enamel sink, the red and black label on Jim's spray can of shaving cream accused me.

In the bedroom, the comforter was still pulled neatly over the sheets. What had changed, essentially? Ultimately, I told myself, my fidelity was to the truth. I stood looking out the bedroom window at Jim's blue Honda Accord, as if it might drive away.

Later, as we lay together in bed, not touching, he asked if I wanted a divorce.

"No. I just want you to love what I love."

"And if I can't?"

"There's something I need out West. Something I want to share."

"Your old life?"

"No."

"Am I crowding you?"

"Not you. This." I waved my hand at the dark, referring to the heavy furniture, the extra bedding in the closet, the street with its bright lights, the expensive cars. "I'm too comfortable."

"I'm not going to be comfortable again for a long time."

"I'm sorry."

"You are?" he asked.

I thought of the sprawling horizon from the lookout tower, the cool electric air, the pulsing power of sex as the lightning illuminated the firefinder. It wasn't about pleasure so much as the feeling of being alive. "I'm sorry for hurting you."

Jim didn't move. "I want to work it out. I don't know if I can, but I want to."

"Me too."

I closed my fingers around his. I put my head on his chest. As he pulled me into his body, another part of me leaned on the catwalk railing to gaze at the view. Big-bellied clouds still held all that electricity, the Seven Devils mountains rising, then plunging, toward Hells Canyon. The sky felt so close I could almost touch the first star, brilliant in its isolation.

SCRAPPY

Sylvie had seen the dog on the wide streets of Crockett many times—yellow, part retriever, with its jaws open in what she had heard other people call a smile, nosing around the dumpsters, waiting at the back doors of the local restaurants, lying on the floor of the old-fashioned five-and-dime that still had a milkshake counter and a proprietor who had named the dog *Scrappy*. She knew the dog. And felt about Scrappy as she had about all dogs since David had died. Sometimes, when she drove down the big hill, heading down Main Street, she saw the yellow dog trotting across the street and wanted to mash him flat with her truck tires.

One morning, *The Crockett News-Messenger* featured

.

Scrappy on the front page, and the girls in Lingerie were talking about it with a customer, a doctor's wife, she guessed, because of the streaked hair and trendy little glasses.

"I have a dog that looks a lot like him," said the doctor's wife, if that's what she was. She fingered a training bra she'd said was for her daughter. The girl had taken up cheerleading and needed some support: such were the woman's problems. "My daughter loves that dog. He's the friendliest thing. I don't understand why nobody takes him home."

Gloriana, who was stacking panties nearby, shifted on her long, skinny legs. "If somebody took him home, I'd miss him." Gloriana was 17 years old. What did she know about loss? "Wouldn't ya'll?" Gloriana gestured toward Sylvie, but Sylvie kept her face arranged in its I'll-be-glad-to-help-you look. She'd seen the dog run up to a little boy just the other day when she was passing by the town park, and of course she'd had to pull over to get her breathing under control. "I'm not much for dogs."

Labor Day morning, she drove through town admiring the store windows mirroring the green hills. The biggest window belonged to *Grand's* where she'd bought a mattress on sale when she first moved to the mountains from the beach, escaping the memories of herself and the baby and Randy tucked into the big bed together on the old mattress. Next door, at *Reasons and Seasons*, she'd found a charm bracelet that now dangled on her wrist: its silver letters spelled out her name, making her feel she was somebody, somewhere; it helped pin her down. Her boyfriend Garrett sometimes took her out for breakfast at *Lou's Diner* across the street. *Alf's Drug*, of course, was on the corner adjacent to the brick courthouse with a big American flag flying next to the blue one for Virginia. She often saw the yellow dog on the sidewalk there, but this morning she guessed there was too much commotion. None of the stores was open yet, but vendors were setting up under tents and awnings for the Labor Day festival. Soon, Main Street would be closed off.

It would mean for a lot of traffic, later on. It would also mean a crowd out at the mall, since schools and government offices were closed and sales were on. The blazers alone had been marked down 25 percent. Summer dresses on a clearance rack were 50 percent off. People would be coming in as soon as the store opened, and probably the work wouldn't let up all day. Home appliances were marked down 15 percent, so she knew Garrett would be busy. He wouldn't have known—and thus could not offer sympathy for the fact—that this would have been her son David's sixth birthday. It was the kind of thing she kept to herself, though alone sometimes, she parked her car across the street from the elementary school and watched the children on the playground, trying to imagine what her baby might be like if he'd lived. He probably would have been among the taller boys, with the tanned, muscular legs of Randy, his surfer father. Today she wouldn't be able to patrol for kids David's age, couldn't even if she wanted to, because of work, and that upset her—she ought to be thinking of David—though another part of her wanted to forget so she could shake off the heaviness in her body.

In fact the usual humidity had lifted, and the air fairly sparkled with vitality, but Sylvie felt ill, her skin clammy, sinuses blocked. She parked in the mall lot and used the employees' entrance near women's wear. As she walked toward the counter, she saw a blonde boy toddling among the racks in a striped shirt. Oh, the soft cheeks and oh the sweet blonde baby hair! She longed to scoop him up. Her heart hammered mercilessly. But then a woman took him by the hand and led him away.

Seeing Garrett at the register in Home Appliances, familiar as toast in his short-sleeved white cotton shirt and dark trousers, nametag pinned to his pocket, was a help. The other girls said that although he had a little salt in his hair and a little bulge at his belt buckle, he was a good-looking man, but of course they'd never seen Randy, with his tanned skin and blonde hair curling to his shoulders, his even white teeth and sinewy body. She and Randy had been high school sweethearts, skipping school together to hang out on the beach, making out in the shelter of the sand dunes. Randy's folks owned a surf shop, so Randy'd naturally gone to work there after graduation, while she put in hours at a dress shop and then quit to have the baby.

In contrast to Randy, Garrett was a dark-haired man with pale skin and dark-lashed eyes who, even, a couple hours after he shaved in the morning, had a five 'o clock shadow. She liked rubbing her cheek against his beard; liked, also, his big hands appreciating the curves of her body (Randy had always wanted her skinnier). He knew how to dress nicely (today's tie was olive and gold, featuring attractive abstract shapes), but he also enjoyed manly kinds of things, like hunting. He'd taken her to get a gun license and given her a pistol after he'd found out what happened to her baby, because he said she ought never again to be unprepared. Together they went to the shooting range so he could show her how to use the pistol. Unlike Randy, who'd had a tendency to run the car out of gas and leave the lawnmower out rusting in the rain, Garrett liked to say, "No use having things if you don't take care of them." He showed her how to clean the pistol and make sure the safety was on so she could carry it safely in her purse. She'd been surprised to find that she could hit the target—not only that, but as Garrett said, she was a damned good shot. Though at first the noise of the pistol's report and the shock of its recoil had frightened her, the earplugs helped, and soon enough, she got used to holding it steady with both hands. In fact, shooting focused the heat in her belly and made her feel strong.

One night after target practice, they'd been sitting on her porch after dark, watching the fireflies, beers in hand, and Garrett had asked, "Why do you want to be out here all by yourself?" She lived about five miles out of Crockett, where she rented a little house up against some Forest Service land. "Aren't you scared of the boogeyman?"

"It's low rent."

"Well it oughta be with that mule path they call a driveway and the pump losing its prime every other day."

"Listen," she'd said.

"Nothing but crickets."

"That's right. No traffic. No barking dogs."

"And a man, but only once in a blue moon." He flicked a piece of lint from his trousers.

"Hon, you know why."

"I respect your losses," he said. "Hell. I'd wonder about you if you'd gone out and rushed into another marriage and had another kid. But sweetheart." He pulled his chair around to face hers and put a hand on her thigh. "It's been two years of you and me, off and on. A man can't feel good about himself when a woman keeps stringing him along."

"You sure about that?"

"Why wouldn't I be?"

"A man your age who never got married? If I wanted you closer, you'd probably run away."

"That what you're afraid of? I'll disappear on you?" He raised her knuckles to his lips. "I'm smarter than that in my old age."

He did have 16 years beyond her, but girls in the store had said even though Sylvie was a doll, with those pretty white teeth and big brown eyes and copper hair down to her shoulders; and even though she had a nice figure and at 23, was of an age to find a younger man; even so, she was the luckiest woman in the place. Linette, whose second husband had left her with two little babies, said, "A nice guy like that don't come along every day."

"I don't feel like he's that much older," Sylvie had responded. "Sometimes I feel like he's younger. He hasn't been through all that much."

"Well, that leaves him more energy for you," Linette replied.

Garrett's mother had died the year before they'd met, but it wasn't the same as what had happened to Sylvie. His mother's death had occurred in the natural order of things, while her son's had been like a punishment for somebody worse than a serial killer. If there was any kind of justice in the world, she had to have been a terrible sinner, but she couldn't figure out what she'd done that was so much worse than anyone else. It made her tired, trying to figure it out. Some days she felt close to a hundred years old, shrunken and rickety.

In the store now, Garrett reached out to touch her cheek with the back of his thumb and said, "How you doin doll baby?"

She turned away. "Been better."

He smoothed her hair with the flat of his hand. "What's the matter?"

"It's gonna be a long day."

"You should've let me come by last night to sweeten you up for it." He looked at her mouth and her neck and the place where she kept the top buttons of her blouse undone to reveal just a little bit of cleavage. He shook his head admiringly. "I could eat you alive."

She brushed her fingers across her forehead. "I've got a headache."

He glanced at his watch. "Lunch break in four hours."

"If we can get away." She nodded toward the aisles, where already a silver-haired man was trying to get Garrett's attention, opening and closing a refrigerator door and glancing pointedly in their direction.

In Lingerie, Gloriana was three customers deep at the register. She turned so the customers couldn't see her mouth when Sylvie joined her and whispered, "This ain't gonna be fun." By lunch hour, the store was buzzing with customers. They flitted from one rack to another, fingering collars and tags, pulling out a bra or slip or nightgown and then putting it on a shelf where it didn't belong. The stack of panties, neatly folded in rows of pastel colors and sizes at the beginning of the day, now looked like a rainbow had exploded. The dressing rooms were full of discarded items off their hangers, some left lying on the floor, others wadded on the benches. Sylvie'd caught one woman coming out of there with a shopping bag full of things she hadn't paid for. The woman put a hand to her bosom and said in a throaty smoker's voice, "I intended to take these to the register. It was just easier to carry them in my bag." When Sylvie called the security guard, and he checked the woman's purse, he found brand new lipsticks and creams from the cosmetic counter, and a watch or two from the jewelry counter as well, but since it was her first offense, he let the woman off. Where was the justice in that?

At noon, Garrett came by to tell her he was taking a fifteen-minute break, but she was behind the counter ringing up a line of customers and couldn't leave. At 1 pm, she managed to go to the ladies room, where she sat on the closed toilet, holding her forehead in her hands, massaging the skin with her fingers. By 2 'o clock, she was dizzy with hunger, so Gloriana took over just long enough for her to run get a soft pretzel and lemonade next door. When the store lights finally flicked at 5 'o clock, warning of closing time, she still had five or six women wandering the aisles, fingering the fabrics, asking her questions about where something might be, how it was sized or whether it would hold up in the washer. Garrett came by as she was finishing up with the last customer. He made as if he was holding a telephone and mouthed the words, "Call you later" as he headed for the double glass doors.

Finally she was locking the register with fingers shaking from exhaustion and relief. In the parking lot, the air was cool, smelling of new mown grass and car exhaust. She got into the truck and rested her forehead on the steering wheel. She could feel knots pulling in the muscles of her back and neck. Her panty hose clung to her crotch uncomfortably, and her hair stuck to her temples. Behind her eyelids there was a feeling of grit, as if she'd been out in the wind.

She put the truck in gear and drove out of the parking lot, preparing to turn right, as usual. But remembering that the main street in town was blocked off for the Labor Day festivities, she decided to take a back way home. It would be nice to pass through the countryside. Since the mall was right at the edge of town, it didn't take long for her to drive from the shopping area onto a road where there were pastures on both sides. The air through the windows felt good, and she was pleased she'd been smart enough to skirt Main Street. She rounded a curve, admiring Price Mountain, its green bulk outlined against the fading sky, then came upon the entrance to the cemetery.

Her son David had been buried behind a white Baptist church out in the country near the Dismal Swamp. Sylvie hadn't visited her son's grave since the funeral. She didn't think she'd find anything she needed under those Virginia pines, mosquitoes lighting on the earth above him, looking for blood he could no longer give. But now, on the occasion of his birthday, she felt like sitting in this quiet place to commemorate the fact that he'd been born. She slowed the truck and turned into the gravel road that led through the Mountain View Cemetery.

The parking lot was empty, so, looking around her and seeing no one, she stripped off her panty hose, peeling them down from under her skirt, then folding them in the truck seat next to her shoes. She locked the truck behind her, then slung the purse over her shoulder. She minced across the gravel road, stones hurting the bottoms of her feet, until she got to the lush grass. She could hear an occasional car on the main road, but otherwise it was still and quiet among the tombstones. She wandered through the grassy aisles, glancing at epitaphs. Most of the dates indicated long lives, old age no doubt the cause of death, and once again she felt the unfairness of David's abbreviated time, remembering the soft baby neck under the fine blonde curls.

There was a faint roaring and she looked up—a jet was going by. David used to stand in the yard pointing up at the Navy jets flying to or from the nearby base. She could watch him from the kitchen window when he was outside toddling between the sandbox and the garden, safe inside their fence carrying his pail and shovel or digging with a stick. She'd taken his safety for granted when they were at home. She and Randy had covered the outlets and moved the heavy bookcases, put up the fence and cleared the yard of garden tools. She hadn't considered that the meter man might leave the gate open for a pit bull that would come in when she had her back turned on a day when the jets were once again flying over, so there was nothing to be heard but the scream of their engines.

Had David called for her? Or had he been knocked over before he could utter a sound? All she knew was when she looked out, the dog had him. It was shaking him like a rag. When it saw her coming with a butcher knife in one hand and a frying pan in the other, the dog ran. She took David in her arms, his little head dangling, and tore off her apron to clot the blood, but his neck was already broken.

That moment went on, as if it were the only moment there had ever been. It was going on now, even as she looked over the gravestones at Price Mountain, and to escape it, she took a step forward and shook her head.

The pulsing that had begun at her temples built to a solid throb. The sound of the jet had trailed off now. Not many flew over Crockett. She sat on a metal bench at the crest of a hill next to a monument that had a big-bosomed angel carved in the stone. She opened her purse and reached for a Kleenex to wipe the tears she felt coming, but they didn't arrive. Instead a dry knot formed at the back of her throat, and though she gazed at the gravestones and tried to make herself cry, instead she imagined taking out her lipstick and defacing all the markers that indicated which dead had lived long lives while others were taken early.

She gathered up her purse without bothering to clasp it shut again and walked to the edge of the trees, where she had a better view of the mountains. Sometimes it helped just to look at them. Today, though, they offered no solace. She was tired. She should go home and collapse. She started back through the cemetery, no longer glancing at the markers but focusing instead on the red of her truck showing through the trees. The truck had been the first thing she'd bought for herself after her divorce from Randy, and seeing it still gave her a feeling that she might be able to flee.

Between her and the road where the truck was parked, the headstones made her think of whitecaps on waves. Randy used to surf those waves; he'd skim across the smooth surface of the water just under the curl, half-crouched, shifting his weight as easily as if he'd been standing on solid ground. He'd tried to teach her, but she'd never been a confident swimmer. When the waves took her inside them, spinning her out of control, she fought to escape, desperate for breath, despite Randy's advice to relax and allow the wave to carry her to shore.

Randy'd had David out on the surfboard before David could walk. She'd stood on the sand watching him hold David up on the board, chubby legs emerging from his orange life vest.

David had squealed, and Randy had hooted, but as the waves rolled toward them, she'd felt her throat close up with fear for the baby's life. "You were always so worried about him," Randy had said. "I can't understand why you didn't check the gate that day." Later, though he assured her he understood it was an accident, a mistake, it could have happened to anyone—even him—he wasn't able to say so looking her in the face. They'd moved out of the house into an apartment, since it was just the two of them again; neither of them could bear David's empty room, the toys tucked into his closet in their old house. But in the apartment, with its smell of fresh paint and new carpet, they'd felt like strangers. As the months passed, each of them going through the motions of eating and sleeping and working, Sylvie still felt like she was in a hospital ward, always in the presence of death. She wasn't surprised when Randy told her he'd found himself loving somebody else—he didn't know how it had happened, but it made him feel alive. He'd said she, Sylvie, would always be important to him. He didn't want to hurt her, but he had to *stay with it*, he said; if David could have told them what to do, he'd have wanted them to *keep on keeping on*.

The red truck she'd bought after that was the opposite of all the little blue Hondas or Toyotas she'd been attracted to in her previous life. Inside it, she drove out of the Tidewater across the Piedmont, until the rolling hills became sheltering mountains that looked nothing like home. What was home anyway? Her parents had sold the house she'd grown up in and moved down to Florida. Her brothers, both much older, had disappeared into their jobs and families, one in California now and the other in North Carolina. It was odd that today in the mountains, she'd imagined seeing whitecaps. Her mind was playing tricks. She blinked her eyes and said to herself, *It's Labor Day in Crockett, you have worked hard.*

A movement at the edge of the trees caught her attention. At first she thought it was a squirrel, but then she saw the yellow head emerge from within the bushes, followed by the re-trieved body. The dog came bounding toward her, its mouth open, tongue dripping saliva. She was tired, so tired she almost didn't care. She looked toward the red truck: it felt distant. The yellow dog was still some yards away, but she thought even at a walk, she'd make it to the truck and get in before the dog reached her. Then the dog sped up, and the distance closed. Though the truck was still distant, she groped in her purse for the keys. But she couldn't find the keys, and the dog was nearing. It had been distracted for a moment by something else, a smell, but now it was back on her path. She felt inside her purse until her fingers closed around the gun Garrett had given her.

The dog bounded toward her again, tail high as a flag. With two hands, she aimed the pistol. Then she felt something come over her, as it did at the shooting range when she aimed at the bulls eye.

"Breathe," Garrett had said. "Let it go when you squeeze the trigger."

When the bullet hit the dog, it, yelped, reared up on its hind legs, and fell on its side. Sylvie did not hesitate but knelt on the ground and dumped the contents of her purse, scatter-ing lipstick tubes and Kleenex, receipts and a comb, until final-ly, at the bottom of the purse, she found the keys. She scooped them up, ran for the truck, and unlocked the door. She sat in the driver's seat with the door closed, looking out the window at the dog she'd shot. It was lying on the ground, its head at an unnatural angle, fur glinting in the fading light between the gravestones. She backed up the red truck and drove fast out of the cemetery, as if the dog were still chasing her.

Garrett's Jeep was in her driveway when she pulled in, and he was sitting in a rocking chair, a six-pack on the porch be-side him, feet up on the rail, tie off and collar undone. She sat behind the wheel of her truck looking at him with the engine still running, considering whether to turn around and drive off someplace until she couldn't drive anymore.

Garrett stood up. "Doll baby?" He set down his beer can and jogged out the dirt driveway until he was at her window. "What took you so long?" He peered into the truck. She'd put the gun down on the passenger seat, among the things that had fallen out of her purse. The purse itself was open on the seat, so it looked like the contents had spilled.

Garrett reached across her lap and turned off the engine. "Wherever you been, it don't look like it did you any good. Come on out and have a beer. You earned it today."

She allowed him to lead her by the hand up to her own porch, where she sat down and drank deeply from the can of Coors he handed to her. She could feel his attention, but she looked off down the driveway that curved down the hill toward the road, shaded by the thick leafy canopy of woods on either side. The bits of sky she could see through the trees were still light: the air was cooling. She could smell the muskiness coming from under the porch, a sharpness from the skunk that sheltered there.

Finally she said, "I went out to the cemetery because today would have been David's birthday."

Garrett put a hand on her knee. "I'm sorry, you know, about the birthday and all. I didn't realize. Maybe you'd rather not have company right now."

She looked down at the bottle in her hands. "I shot a dog out there."

"What?"

"It was running after me."

He held up his palms. "Whoa. Slow down. What dog?"

"It looked like the one in the paper."

"You shot it?"

She nodded.

"Did you kill it?"

"I don't know. I think so."

"Well." He fingered the arm of his rocking chair. "Maybe we better go back and see."

Garrett stood up. "Where'd you leave it?" Then, seeing her face, "You can stay here. I'll come right back."

"No." Sylvie stood, too, and put a hand on his arm. She didn't want to be alone. She looked toward the road. "I feel like it's going to come up the driveway."

Garrett pulled her close. "Not if you shot it." He put his arm around her, and they walked down the porch steps. "Let's go take a look." He sighed. "Been a long day." He kissed the top of her head. "Longer for you than me I guess."

She handed him the keys to her truck. When she opened the door to the passenger side, she scooped everything back into her purse except for the pistol. She sat in the bucket seat with the gun in her lap. Garrett reached across her shoulder to fasten her seatbelt across her lap, and as he did so, he took the gun and put it into the glove compartment. He threw the truck in reverse and backed toward the road.

It was almost dark when they pulled into the cemetery, and as before, there were no other cars to be seen. The tombstones lit up under the glare of the headlights. Garrett took the flashlight, and Sylvie watched as he walked toward the place where she'd left the dog. She could see him stop and squat, as if he were examining something on the ground. After it had killed David, the pit bull had disappeared. Sylvie and Randy drove around looking for it in the alleyways and by the dumpsters, not wanting it to get someone else, but there was no sign.

"Maybe the owners took it out of state so it wouldn't be killed," Randy said.

The air through her open window was beginning to chill.

Sylvie closed her eyes and shivered. When she opened them again, she could see by Garrett's flashlight beacon playing across the road that he was heading back toward the truck. He opened the driver's door. "He's dead, all right. And he is that town dog. I could tell by the white mark on his chest. Too bad." He shook his head. "I don't think he would've hurt you. I think he just meant to be friendly. I know it's hard to tell sometimes. Especially after what you've been through. I don't blame you, but it's a shame. We can't just leave him here. I'll put him in the back of the truck."

"I'll help." Sylvie still wore her skirt and blouse. Her legs were bare, and she had left her shoes on the porch. Because she was so much smaller than Garrett, and guilty, and barefoot, she felt like a child. Once again she felt the sharp stones cut into her feet, but the punishment seemed right. With Garrett, she knelt by the dog and then placed her hands under its head. Though the body was cold, the fur felt silky. "I don't know what came over me," Sylvie said. "They'll want to run me out of town."

"I won't tell nobody," Garrett said.

"There's kids that love this dog. I heard about it at work." She caressed the dog's ears. "They're gonna want to know what happened to it."

Garrett shook his head, releasing his breath. "Doll baby, what would you like for me to do?"

She dug in her purse and found a pen and a napkin. She wrote, "I'm sorry." She tucked the napkin under the dog's collar. "Leave him be. Let somebody find him, and then they'll know where he went."

At work the next day, no one mentioned the dog. It wasn't until she went to Alf's Drug for a Coca-Cola that she saw the collection jar for the Humane Society. A newspaper article about what had happened to Scrappy was pasted beside it on the wall. She put a day's wages in the jar, and the woman behind the counter gave a nod. She was older than Garrett, her hair dyed the color of bricks, with dark red lipstick on two thin, straight lips. "That dog used to come in here all the time." She pointed to a corner, where there was a big round dog bed. "He'd lay right there, good as gold. Maybe you knew him."

"I'm just trying to make something right that'll never be right."

"That's a big job." The woman fingered Sylvie's Coke bottle with bony fingers. "Sure you don't want anything else?" She lifted a hand to the gold cross that hung around her neck.

"What else you got?"

"Hot dogs. Pizza. Fries. Chewing gum. Candy Bars. Chips. You name it."

"Food for somebody on the run." Sylvie shook her head.

The woman eyed her. "You in trouble, hon?"

Sylvie brushed her eyes with the back of her hand. "I lost somebody."

"Oh." The woman's face softened. "I'm sorry."

"My baby. Not even two years old."

The woman's mouth opened and closed.

"What do I owe?" Sylvie asked.

"Not one thing. It's on me."

"I need to pay," Sylvie insisted.

"Mercy," said the woman. "You let go of that purse."

SEX TOYS

In the sorority house, young women crowded together on the couches, in the secondhand chairs, sitting cross-legged on the floor and leaning over the upstairs banister to watch the action below. Jane and Diana, both professors twenty some years older than most of the others, had taken positions on the floor toward the back of the main room, against the wall, while the woman doing the demonstration spoke from a couch by the front door. Jane nudged her friend, who turned, balancing her plastic cup of Margarita in one hand, then followed Jane's gaze toward a side door. "Oh my god," Diana said under her breath. She clutched Jane's forearm as they watched a young woman sit down with her friends near the stairs.

Jane said, "I don't think she's seen me."

The *she* Jane referred to was Ashley, Jane's husband's lover. Ashley tilted her head toward several other young women with shining hair and flawless skin, taut bellies exposed over their low slung jeans, as the hostess made lewd gestures with yet another colorful dildo.

Jane stared. What was Ashley doing at a sex toy party? Wasn't Phillip satisfying her enough? Had he suddenly begun to express a side that was kinky? The most radical sex act she and Phillip had ever performed was lovemaking outdoors, in the woods. True, she'd once declined an invitation, before she met Phillip, to a threesome. It had seemed impossible, like imagining herself using the dildos that were being passed around.

The party hostess had introduced herself as JoAnne. She was seated on a couch covered with a floral sheet and wore a black double-dong around her neck. The double-dong, as JoAnne called it, was a five-foot long, snake-like synthetic dildo with a penis head on each end. Under the white light of the halogen lamp, JoAnne's frosted hair, teased and sprayed, formed a helmet.

She wore a scoop-necked shirt the same rose color as her long curved nails. The shirt clung tight to her fat breasts and to the rolls of flesh beneath them. Her thighs ballooned inside her tight jeans. She held her knees open, gesturing now and then to her crotch, which she referred to as a lily. *This'll get some dew on your lily*, she was saying, holding up a jar of lubricant.

The girls leaned forward with an attention Jane wished they'd muster when she clicked through slides to discuss the history of photography. It wasn't as if, in her lectures, she ignored the contributions of women. Didn't the girls see how Dorothea Lange's images put a female face on American history? Could they not appreciate the pioneering work of Evelyn

Cameron on the Montana frontier? Did they not understand how powerfully the images of Annie Leibowitz presented American icons? What about the women directing films? How could dildos and nipple gel be more interesting than Jane Campion, Sofia Coppola, Robin Swicord?

Jane's friend Diana had been invited to the party by one of her students who was familiar with Diana's research focus on, as her website put it, *the cultural construction of gender and sexuality using the lens of pornography.* The student—Sierra, a pigtailed brunette wearing heavy-framed glasses, wore a plunging neckline and showed considerable cleavage. When they'd first come in, she'd squealed a greeting and ushered them toward the Margarita pitcher.

"Wait'll you see the packaging on this stuff." Sierra poured Margaritas into plastic cups and handed them to Jane and Diana. "You could write three books on dildos alone." When she laughed, a silver ball showed on her pierced tongue.

Diana looked at Jane and shrugged, as if they had no choice but to accept the drinks. As they made their way around the table laden with potato chips, crackers and cheese, and bright orange Cheetos, Jane said, "Could we get in trouble for this?" and Diana replied, "Just be glad you've got tenure."

"What do they want with sex toys anyway?" Jane asked. "They're all young and beautiful. Can't they get the real thing?"

"That's one of my research questions," Diana said.

"Do you think it has to do with AIDS? Are they buying dildos to be safe from penises?"

Diana rolled her eyes. "That's giving them a lot of credit."

To get Jane to accompany her, Diana had to promise she'd lecture Jane's class when Jane was out of town. Locking arms with Jane in Brooks Hall, which housed both Art and Women's Studies at the state university, Diana had said, "If you don't come, so to speak, I'll be the only grown-up there. And anyway, you've been celibate for what, five or six months now?"

Jane nodded.

"So, look, in the absence of the real thing, you can purchase the replacement parts."

"That would be funny if it wasn't so depressing."

"Less trouble than a man," Diana said.

"I liked the real thing."

Diana put her hands on her hips and narrowed her eyes. "You don't know any different."

That day in the hall, Diana had worn what she called her Siren song red knit V-necked dress, which clung to her curves and showed her considerable cleavage. Jane, like her friend, heterosexual, nevertheless admired her friend's creamy flesh and felt plain and awkward beside her, big hands dangling at the ends of her long arms. She took pains to stay in shape, jogging and lap swimming and joining exercise classes, but Diana was the one who never had a shortage of male attention.

"I wish I had half your ovaries," she'd said to Diana.

"Pay attention," Diana had said, "and you can grow yourself another set."

The hostess was passing out order forms and Sierra bounced around, breasts jiggling, to hand out pencils with erasers shaped like penises. Phillip's lover Ashley alternately looked at the order form and talked with the young woman next to her who occasionally handed her a product about which she, apparently, was asking a question. Just now it was the edible underwear. A lamp on the table next to her illuminated Ashley's hair which stood out from her head like dandelion fluff. When she raised an arm, reaching for something, the light shone in such a way that her skin appeared translucent. There was no substance to her flesh except in her breasts. Her face was smooth, without make-up. She had a long, thin nose and ordinary eyes. Jane wondered whether she indeed was a scientific genius, as Phillip had said.

Diana leaned closer, as if to shield Ashley from Jane's view. "Maybe we should wait until everyone starts to leave," she said. "Then we can just blend into the crowd and avoid her."

"I don't want to avoid her," Jane said. She studied the eraser on her pencil.

"What?" Diana said.

"I want to see what she orders."

"No you don't," Diana said. "Anyway, like the hostess just said, the order forms are private."

As they whispered, Sierra, who'd served the Margaritas, tapped Diana on the shoulder. Over the buzz of voices, Jane could hear only pieces of their conversation, something about a Take Back the Night rally and the young woman's boyfriend and a test Diana was planning for next week.

Attempting consolation after Phillip had left Jane for Ashley, Diana had brought over whiskey and cigarettes. Then, as now, she'd worn her black ankle-high lace-up boots, and close-fitting jeans over her sausagey legs, with a tight-ribbed top showed the curves of her voluptuous, middle-aged body. She and Jane sipped whiskey on the purple couch Jane and Phillip had chosen together 26 years earlier, watching flames in the stone fireplace they'd built, carrying stones back from the national forest, over a period of years.

"So what do you think?" Diana asked. "Did he just want someone to suck his cock? Is it a cliché?"

"We had oral sex," Jane said.

"How often?"

"It wasn't at the top of my priority list."

"Good."

"I have work to do, just like he does."

"Even better."

"Isn't it okay for me to have work of my own, and a creative spirit?"

"Bingo Ringo."

"Of course, that doesn't change how I feel. I feel like I failed. Like I'm not enough of a woman."

"Who says?"

The list Jane was holding—nipple gel, French ticklers, dildo with ball bearings, lubricant, clit-warmer—began to blur. Briefly, she resisted a wave of nausea, burying her face in her hands. True, she'd lost interest in supporting Phillip's ego. He, on the other hand, had accused her of wanting everything to be all about her. Was it so wrong to wish one were more interesting to one's spouse than a terrarium full of lizards? But it was all so complicated, since there were, she had to admit, plenty of times she preferred her darkroom to Phillip's company.

Alone a few days after Phillip left and feeling unsubstantial, Jane had taken off her clothes and looked at herself in the mirror. She tried to see herself as she believed Phillip had seen her, examining the loosening skin of her thighs, the new skin tag under her arm. She set up her tripod, put the camera on self-timer, and took a series of digital photographs. Studying them later on her computer, she did not see her Self, but a stranger: the body was a kind of disguise. She'd wanted her photographs to reveal something enduring, but what she saw in her own image was merely flesh. Maybe the essence of Jane could not be revealed in a self-timed photograph.

A few months hence, working through her grief, she'd be photographing dead animals, looking at roadkill and visiting slaughterhouses, biology labs and dog pounds, to capture, as she said in her artist's statement, the essence of life even as it disappeared.

Considering some of what Diana called Jane's pictures of Mr. Death, Diana had said, "You'd talk to me before you offed yourself, wouldn't you?"

"I'm not suicidal."

"Then why do you keep taking pictures of roadkill?"

"So viewers will think about what's gone."

"Why not look at the half-full glass?"

"When I look at full, I think about empty. When I look at empty, I think about full," Jane said.

Searching for carcasses, Jane drove the Virginia mountain roads in new snow and came across a deer magnificent in its bloat. Skillfully, she showed the curves and angles of its frozen repose. It became one of her most acclaimed photographs.

But when she looked at herself in the mirror, she still couldn't see anything but the bags under her eyes, the wrinkled skin of her neck. When Phillip had been doing the looking, she'd believed herself to be kissable, her shoulders like silk. His desire for her had made her feel desirable, yet he, in fact, was the one who'd regularly asked, "What do you see in me anyway?"

"I'm still looking," she'd answered, and it was true. She'd trained her attention on Phillip the same way she trained her camera on everything else. When she took a photograph of something—whether trees in the wind or slaughtered pigs— she did so to examine it later, in the darkroom, where—with her manipulations of chemicals and light—she could bring out whatever emerged. She'd thought it might take a lifetime for her to see the essence of Phillip, for he was as much an observer, with his lizards and video camera, as she with her various subjects and her stills.

In the conversations they'd had since their separation, he'd said, "I just didn't think you ever really got me."

Was Phillip still keeping his late hours at the lab? Had Ashley already grown tired of his long absences? Maybe she wasn't as fond of the lizards as he'd hoped?

Opening her hand to receive a blue dildo with a rotating head of ball bearings, she remembered that Phillip's penis hung a bit crookedly and understood that now, Ashley—a woman not eighteen feet from where she sat—would know about that, his most personal appendage. Jane and Phillip had actually given his penis a name. It was a ridiculous name. Gomer. Maybe he and Ashley had gone to something more sophisticated. Randall, Lewis, Elliott. To be honest, there was a bit of a turn-on in thinking of what the girl might know. The turn-on was not unlike the fascination one might feel watching a shark bite off someone's arm.

She hadn't yet asked Phillip for a divorce.

"Whyever not?" Diana had demanded. "What's the hold up? You've got no children to worry about."

Jane had been very clear, she remembered it vividly, when she and Phillip were still graduate students. "No children, no yardwork, as much art as I can get," she'd told him.

"You sound like you're negotiating a deal, not talking about getting married." Phillip had rolled up the sleeves of his flannel shirt and crossed one blue-jeaned leg over another, resting an elbow on his knee. "I like yardwork." He rubbed his palm up and down one muscular forearm. "I'll do all the yardwork." He'd pushed the Biology book he'd been studying from between them, and reached across the table to squeeze her hand. "You can just be beautiful."

Looking again at the old albums, including photographs in her twenties, she saw that she'd been remarkable for her definitive dark eyebrows in contrast with light auburn hair, her broad-shouldered, narrow-waisted, athletic body, and the serious set of her pretty red mouth. Beautiful? Yes, in the way of the young. Her mother's image was more interesting to her now than her previous self. The shadows under her mother's eyes, the pucker of skin at her lips—there were stories there.

Ashley folded up her deer-like legs and put her arms around them. She leaned her torso forward, compressing her perfect breasts against her knees. The girl was indeed, as Phillip had described her at a Christmas party where Jane had caught him staring at her, "just a stick with boobs." He'd smiled at Jane as she reached up possessively to brush a cracker crumb from his beard, then circled her waist and pulled her close, as she pressed her face into his shoulder.

After he left, she'd rearranged the furniture, packed all the jewelry he'd ever given her into Ziploc bags, and put them at the bottom of her cedar chest. She repainted the walls, transformed them from dark, rich colors to eggshell white. She'd sold their cherry bedroom set and replaced it with contemporary furniture—going for what Diana called the ascetic look.

"You know," Diana had said, shaking her head as she considered Jane's household changes. "This is nice, but you don't have to become a nun."

Jane looked at Ashley now and thought, *Get thee into a burka and go to a Middle Eastern country.*

She was taking a sip from the paper cup when something struck her head hard. She spat out a mouthful of Margarita onto the rug. Everyone was looking at her, and she tried to understand what had happened. The doubledong lay next to her on the floor, forming a U with its two heads. Those who had seen it hit her were asking if she were all right—those who hadn't were trying to figure out the commotion. Jane did not think beyond reflex. She picked up the creature and lifted it, as if in triumph, over her head—for what else was there to do but pretend, at least, to be a good sport? She saw Ashley rise up, her lips opening before she flushed and rocked forward on her stick legs. Jane thought for a moment Ashley would fall forward, but instead she regained her balance and nodded toward Jane, who lowered the creature, one head in each hand, then brought the two heads toward one another, moving them as if they were puppets.

"Hi. My name is Gomer," she said, moving one of the heads. "What's yours?"

"That's a silly name," she said as she moved the other head.

"Well at least it's a name. What's yours?"

"I don't know." She turned the other head down, as if it were sad. "I need a woman to help me decide. How 'bout you?" She directed the question to Diana, who smiled and shook her head slightly. The audience tittered. Jane made the heads move as if they were waving goodbye, then passed the creature on to Diana who kept it moving around the circle.

"Nice recovery," Diana whispered. The thrower of the doubledong, who'd intended a friend to catch it, apologized, and Ashley sat back down, her face red, as JoAnne began to collect order forms.

Diana said, "That was a great exit performance. Now let's get lost in the crowd."

They got up, gathering their purses and slipping their free pencils into their pockets, and went out into the night. It was chilly. The streets were slick. Puddles glistened under the streetlights. The air smelled of wet earth and apple blossoms.

"Want to go get a glass of wine?" Diana asked.

Jane felt dizzy. Maybe Ashley was younger and had a better figure; maybe she was a dynamo in bed; maybe she was able to reflect Phillip in a way Jane never had—but—

"Jane?" a voice called from the direction of the house. Under the front porch light, the friz around Ashley's face was illuminated. She looked like one of the big-eyed sallow-faced children in photographs of refugees.

"Please," Ashley said. "I haven't had a chance to talk to you since—"

Diana took Jane's arm, as if to hold her back, but Jane moved toward the porch.

Under the bare bulb, Ashley's black ribbed tank-top emphasized her inflated breasts, but otherwise she was skeletal, like a house that had been roofed and framed but didn't have walls.

"I just wanted you to know I'm really not an edible underwear type of person." Ashley's voice was surprisingly flat, nasal, nothing like—as Jane had feared—that of a Victoria's Secret saleswoman.

"And this is supposed to make me feel better?"

"I don't know. I just wanted to say I'm sorry."

"What for?"

"For the way things turned out."

"What I mean." Jane felt distant, as if the girl were an actress who'd agreed to answer questions under a spotlight, instead of a human being trembling on a porch step. "Are you actually sorry for anything you did? Is there anything you did that you wouldn't do again?"

Ashley looked away.

"What do your parents say?"

"They don't know yet."

Jane nodded, trying to imagine Phillip as he met a man his own age. He would have to convince the father that he, Phillip, had honorable intentions toward the man's daughter, though he hadn't yet divorced his wife. Possibly the girl's father was younger than Phillip.

"None of it was anything we planned." Ashley gestured helplessly. With her thin lips, her open mouth, her stick-like limbs, the hair making her head look so big, she was like a fledgling.

Jane moved her own weight onto the balls of her feet, tightening the muscles in her calves. She could easily push the fledgling out of its nest, quickly dismantle the girl's illusions, by relating any one of hundreds of intimate stories about herself and Phillip. Did the girl know, for instance, that when they were graduate students living in a trailer out in the county, she and Phillip once found a fox kit that had been hit on the highway and nursed it back to health? They'd bottle fed it together, holding it between them in bed. Phillip had been as young then as Ashley was now. He'd worn his hair in a kind of white man's afro, had a silly thin moustache and a hairless chest. He'd wanted to study mountain gorillas. She'd loved that about him, imagined herself trailing after him, camera gear slung over her shoulders as they'd hack their way through exotic jungles. After he got the PhD and the tenure-track job, lizards had just been a convenience—the kind of thing he could do without much lab space or research money.

Ashley bowed her head. "I just wanted you to know. I wanted you to know we didn't mean to hurt you."

Jane could see goose bumps standing out on Ashley's arms. Maybe Phillip felt protective of Ashley. Maybe being around her made Phillip feel strong. Could a woman not be both strong and lovable to a man?

Jane nodded. "Okay. Now I know."

"There's something else," Ashley said.

Jane waited.

Ashley put her arms around herself and looked at the porch floor. "I really like your photographs."

"Ah," Jane said.

"Nature. You don't romanticize it." Ashley shrugged. "I guess it made me think, well—it made me think you'd be okay no matter what."

"Ah," Jane said again. "I am okay. I'm fine."

"Phillip said you would be." Ashley's voice became eager.

"He says good things about you. He talks about how strong you are. I—" She blushed. "I—don't want to be a photographer or anything, but I'd like to be as—I'm just trying to say—." She tightened her arms around her stomach, as if to ward off a blow. "I don't know if I'll be enough for Phillip. I really don't."

"Look, honey, you're cold out here," Jane said. "You'd better go back inside."

"Are you going to get a divorce?" Ashley asked. She looked toward the door of the house, as if she wanted to run.

"Yes," Jane said.

"I hope I didn't cause—"

"You're a symptom," Jane said. "Not a cause."

"Thank you," Ashley said. Her teeth were chattering.

"You'd be better off as a cause," Jane said. She heard her voice becoming the teacher's. "You need to look at yourself and see what's there."

The rain came down harder as Jane walked toward Diana's car, a red Volvo with rusting fenders. Diana started the engine. It hummed as the windshield wipers moved back and forth.

"You're soaked," Diana said, as Jane closed the car door.

"Sorry. I'm getting the seat all wet."

"I don't care about that." Diana squeezed her shoulder. "Do you want to talk?"

"Not really."

"What would help?"

Jane reached into the back seat for her camera. She took it from its case and looked through the lens at the rain-streaked windows. The camera framed Diana's hands on the steering wheel—each large finger decorated with a different ring.

"Do you still want to go out?" Diana asked.

Even in the dim light, as she moved the camera, Jane could see the puffiness under Diana's eyes, the way her jawline had begun to sag and wrinkle.

"I don't know. What bar in a college town has a clientele over 25?"

"We could set a precedent." Diana reached across the seat to spread her fingers over the lens of the camera. "Come on. Put that down for a change."

Jane lowered the camera. She could smell her friend's apple shampoo and her wet leather jacket. She could see the hairs on Diana's arms and upper lip.

"What were we doing in there?" Jane asked.

Diana reached across the gearshift to touch Jane's hand. "Research."

"What did we learn?"

"Gomer?" Diana laughed. "Did he really call it that?"

Jane let her chin fall toward her chest. "She's just a little girl."

"Maybe its easier for him to deal with her."

"Are you saying I'm high maintenance?"

"I'm saying you're grown up."

"If my life wasn't such a cliché, would it be less painful?"

"Where do you want to go?"

"Somewhere new." She tried to imagine where that might be. The next town over was even smaller than the one they were in. The only thing open would be Wal-Mart.

"We already did that," Diana said.

"Oh yeah."

"You handled a dildo in public. You did not strike your ex-husband's mistress tonight."

"Not much of a story."

"Au contraire."

Jane leaned back against the leather seat. She released the camera into her lap.

"Are you really getting a divorce?" Diana asked.

"I am," Jane said.

"How's that feel?"

Jane lowered the visor and looked in the mirror. "Like I can finally see myself."

"What about me?" Diana asked.

She turned, laughed, pinched the flesh on Diana's upper arm. "Substantial."

"So where do you want to go?"

Jane settled into the seat, closing her eyes. The muscles in her neck unclenched. She felt the car jerk forward as Diana engaged the clutch. Diana shifted again, and Jane's eyes flicked open. The blurry windshield looked just like her images when they began to emerge from the chemicals in the darkroom. She wasn't outside looking in this time, but inside soupy shapelessness on the photographic paper. "Did you order anything?" Jane asked Diana.

"Not yet, but I have the form. There's packaging I want to study." Diana glanced at Jane. "Why? Do you want something?"

"What if we set some of it up in my studio?"

"No more roadkill?"

"We paste wings on a dildo, you hold it, and I call it—"

"Bird in the hand."

Jane laughed. "Bingo ringo."

WOMEN WHO SLEEP
WITH ANIMALS

That midsummer day, as I trotted after my cat through the woods, a bearded man appeared at a bend in the trail, wearing a red T-shirt and blue shorts. He gave the impression of shapeliness and vigor. A full head of hair and beard on a thick neck. Wide shoulders narrowing to a trim torso. Muscular hips and shapely legs. Wow. As the man came into focus, I realized I knew him. Tim…but his last name was gone. I'd met him and his wife Shelley at a dinner with mutual friends. Shelley, who had Multiple Sclerosis, sat in a wheelchair, and I'd been impressed by the way he treated her—not like an invalid.

I was calling, "Wipey," the open cat food can in one hand. It was time for her medicine. Wipey was so named because she had frequent bladder infections and a habit of wiping her crotch on the rug, sometimes leaving behind brown stains. That, among other things, had driven my husband of 29 years, Roland, away. We'd been divorced for a year. Since then, I'd had no other relationships. Roland, on the other hand, had several. Though his affairs had been a preoccupation for me, all right, they weren't just then, as I crunched through the dead leaves, inhaling the musky odor of Appalachian detritus. "Wipey," I called, watching the calico's tail disappear around a bend in the path, as if she were playing a game of hide-and-seek.

"Tammy?" Tim slowed to a walk. "Are you a trail runner, too?"

"Only when I can't find my cat."

"Can I help?"

The two of us crackled through the fallen leaves, calling, "Kitty kitty," Tim going one direction, me the other. I felt bad. I imagined Tim had only so much time when Shelley didn't need him, and here he runs into, like my daughter would say, a crazy cat lady. But lo and behold if, when we converge, he isn't holding my stinky little kitty.

Wipey cuddled up to him like he was the one who fed her every day, cleaned her litter box, and gave her the medicine she needed.

"You have the touch," I said.

"We have a cat ourselves."

"Only one?"

"How many do you have?" he asked.

"Nine."

He gave a little laugh. "No shit." He handed her over, and Wipey meowed, like she wanted to return to him.

"You guys live around here?"

He pointed up the hill. "Almost at the top."

"What's Shelley up to?" Then I felt myself blush, wondering if "up to" was really the best choice of words, since Shelley couldn't get up.

"Shelley's playing the market," Tim said. "As usual."

"What's that, some online game?"

"She's a day trader. You know, Wall Street."

"You can do that in Crockett?" I imagined Shelley, her head fallen to one side, managing her keyboard with her one good hand.

He nodded. "You'd be surprised what you can do in Crockett." He gave a sly grin. "What about you?" he asked, looking through the trees as if for my house.

"I'm just a few minutes that way." I pointed.

"I've heard about your paintings," he said. He didn't seem to be in a hurry.

"You want to come see?"

"Sure."

In the house, all nine of my cats appeared one by one and rubbed against his ankles or jumped into his lap while I was boiling water for his tea. He sat in front of *Spice-scape*. Floor to ceiling, the painting is ten feet tall and six feet wide. Tim gazed into the yellow rectangular spice containers with their red caps opening into a dreamscape of animals: red and blue-checkered elephants with big blue third eyes; a giant tabby cat, curled tail around paws. In the front left corner, a many-armed African goddess danced. A mountain sheep nudged her crotch while she embroidered Michelangelo's Adam. In a corner of the canvas coiled a rattlesnake of colored threads.

He pointed toward Adam. "Looks like the dark goddess pulls the strings on the white man."

"True enough."

He laughed. "Shelley would like this one." He blew the heat from his tea and got up, strolling around the house, looking at my paintings.

"You want to bring her by?"

He looked at me naked—that's how I described it later

to my good friend Jordan, who lives down the road. Jordan, single herself for five years after two failed marriages, who's dyed her hair black and lost 20 pounds on her Weight Watchers diet, is always after me to try online dating. We met in a yoga class.

"Anyone can look at anyone that way," I'd explained to her as we walked in the woods. "It's not about sex, it's about availability. He was making himself available to me." I made her stop in her tracks, took her by the shoulders and said, "Like this." I looked at her like I usually do, without hiding anything, but she didn't get it.

"It's different between girlfriends," she said. "Married men aren't supposed to look at us like that. The guy wants to get laid."

But that afternoon at my house, Tim said, "How 'bout if I bring Shelley by next Sunday?"

I can admit to you now, though I didn't to Jordan, I thought about Tim, all right. My ex-husband Roland was sleeping with this woman and that, why shouldn't I sleep with this married man and that? Roland and I had lived out of town in a cabin by Stony Creek for most of our married lives. Since our kids had left home, and Roland had retired from his longtime job as forest manager, he'd been changing into someone else. In the end, he'd kicked all nine of the cats outside. I remember he was lying on the couch just after that, while several of the cats sat on the window ledge, making eyes at us from the cold. When I objected, he'd said, "I'm not an animal. I'm a man. I want to live like one."

"Men are animals," I reminded him.

"Don't give me that feminist crap."

"Women are animals, too."

"I'd like to be able to walk to town and get a cup of coffee," he said.

"I'll make you coffee," I said.

"That isn't the point."

He'd come to hate the mulch pile (too messy), the wood-stove (inconvenient). The TV and VCR (time to upgrade to a better system). The truck we used to haul firewood and ma-nure (weren't we old enough to drive a real car by now?).

"I've grown up," he'd said. His eyes were dull. He'd shaved the long beard he'd worn all our married lives, and his chin looked obscene to me, like a body part not meant to be ex-posed—pale, puffy, mottled. He'd been a Forestry major when we'd met in college, and I loved the way he knew the trees, but management had soured him. When his father died, leav-ing him an inheritance, Roland gave me the house and bought himself a place in town and a BMW. He was still a pretty good-looking man, and he went around with younger women who went to aerobics or weightlifting instead of yoga.

Unlike Jordan, I hadn't been looking for a boyfriend. I'd let all the cats back in, and they kept me warm at night, in the crook of my knees, at the hollow of my back. I painted and kept in touch with the kids, grew Echinacea and goldenseal I sold at the Farmer's Market.

Yet after Tim came over that day, remembering his boy-ish body, the curve of his ass in those silky running shorts, the muscles in his calves, and that clean, open naked look he gave me—although it was true what I'd said to Jordan about the look, it was innocent, and when I thought of it, the sexual urges went out of me—still, I envied my cats the comfort of nestling into Tim's manly lap, feeling the stroke of his fingers. As the cats purred around me in my bed, I cupped my own breasts in my hands. Roland had liked them. I liked them, too—they balanced my hips. They weren't feeding any babies anymore, but I remembered the pleasure when Roland had touched them—a thought that sent heat to my groin and made me moan until Black-Black, my oldest cat, looked up at me as if to say, "Honey, get over it."

When Tim brought Shelley to my house, I watched him look at her with pure unadulterated love, the real thing. He was like a door opening onto a flower to let in the light toward which she yearned. He wheeled her around to see my paintings, positioning her just right so that—though she couldn't completely lift her head—she could see everything she wanted, and then, since it was getting on evening, I offered some wine. We sat on the front porch listening to the crickets and the creek.

They asked the usual questions—what were my influences as a painter, how'd I find this great house, how long had I lived here, how high did the creek get when it rained hard, what kinds of birds and animals had I seen in the forest around us. All the things I wanted my kids to appreciate, Tim and Shelly did. All the things that drove my kids crazy—the cats, the smells, the stains on the rug—they didn't seem to mind. (My kids, like their father, had gone terminally suburban.) After a while Shelley, sitting next to me, put her one mobile hand on mine, and said, "Tammy, this is the best time I've had in months."

"Me, too," I said, though I wasn't entirely sure it was true. I liked being by myself with the cats.

"Being in the public schools for so long, I had to listen to a lot of noise. Now I can't get enough quiet."

"Quiet is good," I said.

"When you're confined like I am, your mind wants all the freedom it can get. It's great to be around a freethinker like you are. A real artist."

"My ex didn't think so, and my kids aren't so sure."

"You know I was a drama teacher, right?"

I nodded.

"I'd like to stage a show right here. Right on your lawn."

"I'm game."

Shelley said, "What do you think, honey?"

"All the world's a stage," he said. "As long as it doesn't upset the apple cart."

"Upsetting the apple cart's what it's all about," Shelley said.

Shelley went on drinking wine, but Tim switched to water. Too much wine gave me a headache, so I slowed down, too. If Shelley wanted to get drunk, though, I sure wouldn't stop her. The moon came up. Tim went to the bathroom.

Then Shelley said, "I worry about him, you know."

"Why?"

"He's a healthy man."

"He looks healthy."

"He likes you, you know."

I smiled. "I like him, too."

"More importantly," she said, cocking her head so she could make eye contact in her sideways fashion. "I like you."

"Well, that's mutual."

"I want to give you a gift."

"There's no need for that."

"I wouldn't say this if you weren't an artist." Shelley tapped me on the arm. "Artists are unshockable, you know."

I laughed.

"I want you to do me a favor."

"Your gift to me is a favor to you?"

She smiled. "Touché."

I put my hand on her good shoulder. "I'm glad to do you a favor, Shelley."

As I withdrew my hand, she took it in her one good hand. Her head, lolling to the side, kept her eyes focused downward, but when she squeezed my fingers, I took it as a good sign.

"Can you—would you—be with Tim?"

"I'm with Tim and you right now."

"No." She took a deep breath. "I mean—sleep with him. Make love."

I sat there for a minute, getting my bearings. She was wrong if she thought I was unshockable.

She released my hand, used it to lift her wine glass from the table, and managed to take another sip.

"You want me to, let me get this straight—I—"

"Let him think it's his idea. It's okay with me. I've told him he can." With careful deliberation, she put her wine glass down. The frogs had started up their nightly chorus, and the air smelled of woodsmoke. "I like you. You're perfect. Give him a chance." Raising her eyes to mine, though her head was inevitably crooked, she smiled. "You'll pardon me for this, but I think he could do you a favor, too. Call it symbiosis."

Before I could think how to respond, Tim came back and sat down beside her. He raised the wine bottle, his eyes asking me a question, and I felt myself blush. "No more," I said.

As they were leaving, I leaned down to give Shelley a hug, and whispered into her ear, "Thank you, but I really can't."

Summer mornings are steamy in the mountains sometimes, and I like to sit on my porch with a cup of coffee and a cat on my lap, watching the fog burn off. I can hear the creek rushing over stones and feel the water in the air weighing down my clothes. Some mornings the fog's so thick, I can't even see the mailbox at the end of my driveway. Other times, the fog's a wispy live thing moving from the dip at the bottom of the road going toward town to the trees in the hollow by the pond where the deer gather just before daylight. It's cool those mornings, though later in the day, it gets so hot I have every shade drawn and every fan running. But that July day, still cotton-headed from sleep, I had a shawl over my shoulders and was glad for Pookie's warm gray self in my lap. It's a time of day when I am of no mind, meaning there are no thoughts of past or future, only fog in my visuals, rocking chair under my

butt, and two hands around my warm mug. Desire was con-
spicuously absent, and what was going on in the world wasn't
getting my attention. A squirrel chattered, some doves cooed,
and a blue jay swooped down to raid the feeder. Through the
fog, a dark apparition moved along the road toward the house,
taking shape, becoming, finally, Tim himself, in all his running garb glory.

"Hey," I said, expecting him to run on by, but he slowed to
a walk and came into the yard.

"You're up early."

"It's a good time to contemplate."

"Am I interrupting?"

"I'm not exactly—dressed." I indicated my robe.

He laughed. "Not a problem."

"Coffee?"

He shook his head. "Don't get up. Your cat looks too comfortable." He stepped up onto the porch as if he'd lived there all
his life. "Just tell me where it is."

Pretty soon he was sitting next to me, the two of us like
old folks in our rockers who'd been meeting for coffee every
day.

Tim pointed to the branches of the oak tree by the
porch. "Indigo bunting. You can see him, right there." He
got up stealthily, stood next to my chair, put an arm around
me and directed my head until I saw the bright blue body of
the bird moving through the tree branches.

Tim smelled of deodorant and sweat. His hand rested easily on my shoulder. He gave it a squeeze. "I'm surprised you
have as many birds as you do, with all your cats," he said. "I'm
glad to see you have them belled."

As if on cue, Pookie shifted in my lap, making the bell
around her neck tinkle.

"I believe in giving critters a chance," I said.

"That makes two of us." He made a "Hm" sound—as if

he'd just thought of something else, and briefly laughed. "No, three. Shelley's among the greatest fans of chance-giving I've ever met." He dropped his hand from my shoulder, easily, then shook his head, smiling. "She gave *me* a chance. And—I remember when she was teaching—she had this student. Greta Early. Overweight, bad skin, no talent. Somehow this girl gets the nerve to audition for the high school play, and Shelley finds her a part. Every year Shelley used to 'gift' somebody, somebody who'd otherwise be a loser. It's—or anyway it *was*—her approach to education. The other kids must've thought Shelley was nuts, but she just kept telling this girl how good she was. Shelley said it works. Sometimes I wonder if she was gifting *me* when she agreed to get married."

His praise of Shelley went through my body like an electric pulse. When a married man loves his wife, and I know it, I let down my guard. As I relaxed into my enjoyment of his tenderness toward Shelley, I felt a surge of desire. His proximity, his conversation—now this opening into the blooming garden of husbandly love—all went into my brain and massaged something. I felt myself flush.

"You okay?" he asked.

I fanned myself. "Oh I still get hot flashes."

"I wish I could work up a sweat just sitting there." He smiled, checked his watch. "Instead I have to run. I'm only halfway there."

"Give Shelley my best."

He nodded, leaned down, and kissed me on the cheek.

Maybe I should say that I like my religion sensual—that's why I built my altar with the figures of Buddha and Shiva and Ganesh as well as incense, candles and a figure of Mother Mary covered in Mardi Gras necklaces. I don't believe we're born sinners. I've looked in the eyes of my newborns and there, I saw only blankness and other-worldliness that came from a place I could no longer remember. If there were such things as right and wrong, wrong was whatever separated us from our best selves, which some people call God. Whatever interfered with my ability to live well, see clearly, and be in the present moment—that's what I wanted to avoid. Desire, as our yoga teacher Blanche so often reminded us, was not exactly wrong, but it could keep us from awareness, it could place us in an unattainable future with a vision fueled by a kind of stupor that kept us drunk on fumes instead of sustaining us with real nourishment. In her yoga class, as I held the warrior pose, I looked in the mirror at my own form—still vigorous in yoga pants and a tank top, graying hair cut in a bob at my jaw. I was full breasted, middle-aged-waisted, and freckle-armed with my redhead's complexion. With my green eyes, I wanted to see things as they were.

Shelley called a few days after Tim stopped by. "Can you come Saturday night for dinner?"

I felt my throat tighten. What did Shelley really want? Black-Black balanced coolly on the arm of a chair, then stretched forward, lowering her head over front paws with claws digging into the upholstery, mouth open in a yawn that showed her pink tongue. She was a cat doing downward dog. When I did that pose in yoga class, Blanche said, *Find your center, breathe from your center. Don't look at anybody else. Go inside. Find what you want in the pose. Now forget about it. Don't think. Just lengthen and breathe.*

I'd used yoga during labor with Theresa, my second baby. When the pains came, I practiced the breathing that had relaxed me in yoga poses and visualized the opening cervix, just as I'd learned to visualize lengthening muscles in my lower back during the downward dog pose. It worked so well, my cervix was dilated in no time flat, and my labor took all of two hours.

I felt my muscles unclench and asked Shelley what I might bring to the table.

In the grocery store, picking up blueberries for the pie I intended to make for Tim and Shelley, I saw Roland, my ex, with his newest girlfriend. She led a little boy by the hand as Roland pushed the cart in the frozen food aisle. She wore jeans and a tight ribbed top that showed her athletic figure. Roland, newly muscled from the gym—his second home after he retired—wore shorts, athletic shoes, and a T-shirt. He was like a man connected to the woman by an invisible rope—when she stopped, he stopped. When she looked to her right or her left, he followed suit. But I liked what I saw in *her* posture—a kind of independence, as if she could take or leave Roland, and while she was responsible to the child, she would not allow him to lead her this way and that. The boy and the man both looked to her for direction.

Still, the curve of her waist and hips, and the little boy as evidence of her fertility made me feel my age. My lower back tightened and caught, as if in response to a fist in the belly.

As I hurried to the checkout before they could see me, the words *she's all dried up* came into my mind, as if I'd been a river that now was in drought, depriving the entire community of a necessary resource. When I was going through the change of life, I'd made my own drawings of the uterus before and after the change, contemplating the drama within. The diagrams always looked to me like a steer's skull—the fallopian tubes were the longhorns, the ovaries were the ears, the uterus narrowing at the cervix and opening to the vagina formed its head. Where once my steer's head was dropping eggs, now it was simply an artifact. When I got home, I cried. There was no use stopping it. As I lay on the couch, sniffling and wailing and staring at the ceiling, Pookie made a bed on my belly, Black-

Black sat on the window ledge, calmly licking her paws. Wipey sniffed her anus and gave it a desultory lick.

Eventually I got up. I made the pie. I cleaned up Wipey's newest brown streak on the rug, took a shower, put on a sundress, and got myself over to Tim's and Shelley's for dinner.

We ate grilled salmon, green beans and tomatoes with basil from their garden. We put ice cream on my blueberry pie. After dinner, we sat on their deck sipping brandy. The house was situated high enough on the mountain for a view into the valley over the trees. Tim and I were in comfortable wooden deck chairs, set close together, and Shelley had parked her wheelchair on the other side of Tim. He rested a hand on her thigh. I wondered if she could feel it. The warm rush of alcohol made me dizzy.

"How long have you been in the wheelchair, Shelley?" I asked.

"Five years now?" she asked Tim.

He nodded. "About that."

He kept touching me," she said. "It helped. When you're in a wheelchair, people don't look at you. You feel invisible. Touch is important."

I rubbed the back of my neck. "Yeah. I miss that myself."

"No boyfriend?" Tim asked.

I shook my head.

"How 'bout a masseur?" he asked.

"Can't afford it."

Tim got up, stood behind me and put his hands on my shoulders. With his fingertips, he rubbed my temples.

The insects are loud sometimes during a Virginia summer, and the chorus came up as we sat outside in the darkening woods. With the brandy warming my insides and Tim rubbing my shoulders and neck, I dissolved into something that vibrated, hummed, and chirped along with the creatures of the forest. Shelley, I assumed, was buzzing into blurriness with her brandy, but as the first stars glittered through the hazy humid sky, her voice came out of the dark. "Just sitting here, sometimes I'm bored out of my tree, but what I *can* still do is orchestrate things. I'm a director. I direct my *own* plays. The drama is in the here and now. I like to push my characters, see where they'll go." Her words were slurring a little. "Tim's seen it before, haven't you, hon?"

Tim's hands stopped moving on my neck. "Like at Hank's?"

"I pushed your buttons."

"She got me so mad, I put my fist through my brother's wall."

My muscles were loosening, my jaw unhinging. "That doesn't sound like you."

"Oh, it's him all right," Shelley went on. "Tim buries his feelings. He was letting his brother push him around. I said just enough to open it up for him."

"Pandora's box," I said. "That was a while back, I bet."

"A couple of years," Tim said. His fingers moved expertly down the back of my neck, my shoulders, found a knot by the shoulder blade, and worked it out.

"At least I didn't break any bones," Tim observed.

"My words have a lot of power," Shelley said.

Tim's fingers dug a little too hard.

"When you can't move, you see more, you hear more," Shelley said.

"I can imagine," I said. Tim's fingers went up into my hair now, massaging my scalp.

"Touch her all you want, Timmy boy. She's enjoying it."

"I can't disagree," I said. "But if you're getting tired—"

"He's not tired, he's turned on," Shelley said.

Tim dropped his hands from my shoulders. "Honey, I think you're a little drunk. How much have you had to drink?"

"He thinks he's in control, but he's not," she said. "He does everything for me, all the time. Down to wiping my butt. What do I get to do for him? It's uneven. The owing is all on my side. If you two care about me at all, you'll—"

I stood up. "Maybe I should go."

"No." Shelley's voice was thick. "Oh, Timmy, please just kiss her."

Tim stepped toward me, reaching for me, and I was just drunk enough to half step, half fall into him. He kissed me on the lips, as you might kiss a sister, then looked at her. "How's that?"

"More," she said. "Put your hands on her ass. Touch her breasts. Put your tongue in her mouth. Come on. She's a woman. You need to be a man."

"Shel," he said. He knelt in front of her wheelchair and put his head in her lap.

"She wants you to," Shelley said.

I stood awkwardly looking down at them, buzzed enough to be slow-headed and swaying, arms dangling, my neck and scalp and lips still warm from Tim's touch. Tim turned slightly to look at me, as if to ask me what I wanted, or was he begging me to go home?

My tongue felt thick. "You're a great masseur," I said.

He reached out a hand. An invitation. A single lamp illuminated an empty chair in the house behind him, while around us the dark pressed in, fragrant and humid. I could feel the dampness under my arms, beneath the hair on my neck. I touched my fingers to Tim's. I could imagine everything— the two of us falling into each other, mouths opening, my lips at his neck, his hands traveling under my shirt touching my breasts. The abandon with which each of us would pull off the other's clothes, our mindless groping, the smell of him aromatic as wet earth.

Shelley's eyes were on our hands. "You can use the guest

bedroom. There's nothing to be afraid of." Shelley's voice was shrill. She crumpled in her wheelchair like a wilted plant, observing the action atilt.

Tim's hand was warm, the palm soft, about the same size as my own. His thin gold ring pressed against my palm. Nothing else changed—the frogs still croaked, the air pressed in around us, thick with the smell of citronella candles Shelley had lit to keep away the mosquitoes. I took a breath of that air and felt heat emanate from my groin, traveling up my spine and out my right arm to the hand in Tim's. I squeezed. My head buzzed with confused thoughts, but one seemed clear: he was a man I liked. I felt good will travel between us, enjoyed a hormonal surge, and opened my palm. "Great dinner," I said. "If there's more dessert to be had," I looked at Shelley, "it's yours."

"The night is young," she said, but Tim nodded appreciatively, one hand on his wife's shoulder.

As I descended the steps to their yard, I was careful to hold the railing. From there, I made my way around their house to the driveway and out to the road. I'd neglected to bring the flashlight, but my feet found the pavement, even with the brandy in my belly. Above the insect's buzz, I heard an owl hoot, and on the state highway, a distant whisper of traffic.

At home, I moved Pookie and Black-Black off my bed so I could turn down the covers and get in. Once I did, they jumped up again and settled close. The vibrations of their purring were like the engine that drove the whole world. My body responded with its own kind of pleasure, synapses firing messages of comfort. The heat in my groin was gone. Desire, I understood, was the tip of a cat's tail disappearing around a corner. I rearranged my pillows—one under my head, one at my back, another between my legs. I pulled the blanket up to my neck, and snuggled next to my cats, easy with the mammalian familiar.

LISA NORRIS is the author of WOMEN WHO SLEEP WITH ANIMALS (Stephen F. Austin University Press, 2011). Her previous story collection, TOY GUNS, won the 1999 Willa Cather Fiction Prize and was published by Helicon Nine Press. Her stories, essays and poems have been published in many literary journals, most recently *Shenandoah, Ascent, Blueline, South Dakota Review, Toad,* and *Smartish Pace.* She received a B.S. in Fisheries and Wildlife from Virginia Tech, M.A. from Idaho State University, and M.F.A. from American University.

After teaching as an instructor at Virginia Tech for 15 years, she moved to Ellensburg, Washington, where she is an Associate Professor at Central Washington University. At home, she—like her many of her characters—finds comfort in her mammalian elements.